Advance Praise for
REVOLUTION EMPIRE

"Filled with concepts and challenges so increasingly familiar in today's chaotic world, *Revolution Empire* presents a thought-provoking and inspiring lesson into the often brutal truth of absolute power and the preciousness of the freedom that can defeat it."

—**April Thome**, Director, KATS; Founder of HomeLink Yakima, a leading homeschool curriculum, training, and support program

"Serious though its themes are, *Revolution Empire* is above all entertaining. Highly readable. It will find a big audience and so its ideas will be deservedly spread wide. Stories like *Revolution Empire* give us hope that the young will leave behind a better world than that which previous generations have handed them."

—**Geale Peter Lawrence**, Author, Screenwriter, Producer

"*Revolution Empire: Book One* is an immersive and quite subversive tale.... To pull the reader deep into a web of dystopian oppression and thrilling intrigue, Rob has created a strange new world that will be eerily familiar to careful readers and students of history.... By the conclusion of Book One, readers will be eager to join forces with Donovan the Sewer Rat as they learn one of life's most important lessons, 'Freedom is not given. It is taken.'"

—**H. Kirk Bozigian**, Practitioner Faculty of Marketing, Providence College; Former Vice President of Marketing, Hasbro, Inc.

REVOLUTION EMPIRE

BOOK ONE:
HISTORY NEVER RETREATS

REVOLUTION EMPIRE

BOOK ONE:
HISTORY NEVER RETREATS

ROB TRAVALINO

PERMUTED
PRESS

A PERMUTED PRESS BOOK

Revolution Empire:
Book One: History Never Retreats
© 2023 by Rob Travalino
All Rights Reserved

ISBN: 978-1-63758-995-3
ISBN (eBook): 978-1-63758-996-0

Cover art by Cody Corcoran
Interior design and composition by Greg Johnson, Textbook Perfect

PERMUTED PRESS

Permuted Press, LLC
New York • Nashville
permutedpress.com

Published in the United States of America
1 2 3 4 5 6 7 8 9 10

For Tina, my muse.

CONTENTS

Those who cannot remember the past are condemned to repeat it.

—George Santayana, *The Life of Reason*

1

REQUIEM FOR A RAT

T'Empire...
  Seems like it's been here fo'ever. T'was here long 'fore I was born and t'will be here long af'er I'm dust.

HUDDLED UNDER A NARROW SLASH of dim and dust-filled light in a debris-strewn alley, seventeen-year-old Donovan Washington Rush scribbled the words across the dry and yellowed parchment pages of a small hand-bound journal. *Everything written,* he thought to himself, *nothing digital where "Boss Man's" eyes could find it.* Though hiding carefully, and clearly worried about discovery, Donovan penned his words slowly and deliberately. The book once belonged to his father, Dr. Princeton Rush. It was his journal, and this was the very first time that Donovan had dared add to it.

The weathered book was filled with words on escape, freedom, tyranny, and rights—the very kind of ideas that a lowly Sewer Rat had been conditioned to never fully understand. As far as most in

1

the Sewers knew, these were all exclusive to the Empire. They were dangled as gifts that could be bestowed or taken away on Imperial whim. According to Dr. Rush, it wasn't always so. The Empire had hijacked these words and concepts and changed their use and made them property, condemning their original intent to die off like the aging witnesses of a long-ago war, once gone, their lessons forgotten and buried with them.

That said, the hand-written journal still had two distinct sets of interpretations, and Donovan had initially considered them both. Either the tome was filled with the delusional rantings of a madman or it was a stroke of absolute and forbidden genius. Once enticed by the latter, Donovan had shared some of the words with his closest and most trusted friends, those he grew up and survived with. Together, they had built a kind of secret order based on the writings, one that had spread through the shadows of Donovan's land. They named themselves the Brothers and Sisters of the Sword, and they adopted the slogan "Freedom or Death." It was dangerous stuff—subversive, yet possibly entirely pointless. Regardless, Dr. Rush's journal would forever be precious to Donovan. It was the only thing his father had left behind before he vanished into the very same shadows that Donovan now clung to for protection.

Dr. Rush wrote that his journal was full of secrets worth dying for. That meant the book contained secrets that, if true, were worth killing for as well. Still Donovan had read every line, absorbed every passage and illustration, notation, crease, and fold until he finally reached the point where he felt comfortable adding his own marks next to his father's.

Sensing people approaching from the jagged, street shadows beyond, Donovan finished making his marks, surreptitiously knowing that the mere act of writing was a punishable offense.

Even here in the relative security of darkness, Donovan knew he was being watched, not just by the all-seeing eyes of the Empire he wrote about but by something far more insidious. He knew he was being watched by many of the people themselves, looking through the lens of the Empire's carefully engineered fear of reprisal that was drilled into them. *They, too,* Donovan thought, *are the Boss Man's eyes.*

As Donovan ducked down to hide his face under an angled tricorne hat pulled low, he thought about how he had chosen those first words and his motivation for writing them. Like his father before him, Donovan expected to vanish for what he knew and meant his new inscriptions for anybody that followed his path, for those who'd remain after he was gone. The teen also knew that, like his father had stated, the words meant nothing unless put to action. If his father had indeed risked death, only by taking the same risk could Donovan find the truth and power, if any, behind the words.

Before moving on to his next illicit sanctuary, Donovan stopped to dwell on the book's cover. It was aged, pitted, and stained, the leather grain filled with dirt and grease of time and human touch. *How many hands?* Donovan wondered. *How many minds have pondered the words inside? Has this book made any difference at all to anybody before me, or are they just ghosts long since devoid of power over human affairs?*

Donovan continued to run his fingertips over the volume, stopping at the center of the cover. Scarred into the leather by firebrand was a crude, slashed form of a raised palm with a star emblazoned in the center. He studied how it was carefully filled in with gold paint, rubbed by hand into the deep marks to preserve them with meaningful purpose and reverence. *And what of the single word that had been burned across the palm? What of Libertatem?*

After scanning and rescanning the dark cobblestone streets beyond him, Donovan flipped backwards through a handful of dog-eared pages and paused at a series of carefully hand-drawn maps. Like the book's cover, both maps and pages were badly faded and worn, every word and image rubbed dim by the repeated touch of his and his father's hopeful fingers. Whether the words were true or not, they offered something quite unique to Donovan's world—they offered hope.

The initial target of the teen's attention was the one map that detailed his present location, a long straight thoroughfare marked Regent Street, one of the area's oldest. Using it as a guide, Donovan pointed the tip of his pen to the Northeast Quadrant of the Under City. Regent Street was only three Under City blocks from a darkened and nondescript area that Donovan's father had noted as "Perimeter Five." That was the boy's destination, the place where his father's cryptic breadcrumbs seemed to lead. A series of arrows then directed Donovan to turn the page to the next group of maps showing Perimeter Five in more detail.

Even in simple map form, the area seemed darker and more foreboding. A tangled grid of streets was left unmarked; shapes and buildings and landmarks were hastily sketched as if done from memory or on the fly. If Perimeter Five was Donovan's main goal, it was an uncertain one at best. As for what came after, it seemed only his father knew. Surrounding the diagrams of this shadowy place, Dr. Rush using his old quill pen like a knife had dug two hard notations into the paper. The first read, "Black Flag," with an accompanying death's head and crossbones. The second notation had the same star and palm from the book's cover. Next to it was the same word: *Libertatem*. Next to that was a tiny drawing of what looked like the lower part of a statue—specifically, just the legs below the knee. *Freedom either didn't or couldn't run anymore,* Donovan thought. *Neither can I.*

Looking into the dank malaise of Regent Street, Donovan took in the musty air and dingy sights of the only world he'd ever known. There was no observable sky, but massive dirty icicles hung from immense nondescript structures far above. Donovan wondered, *Is that the very boundary of the Empire? If so, it's a fitting sight.* The massive ice spires seemed like the foreboding and deadly daggers of some great trap poised to smash down on anybody who dared ponder what was out of reach. Icy and putrid meltwater rhythmically dripped from the massive stalactites and down to the hot cobblestones below where it formed into brackish puddles of germ-infested wastewater. The steam from the cooling water in turn created an eerie, accompanying ground fog.

Just above this dank atmosphere, ancient four and five-story brownstones and low, rickety wooden tenements leaned into each other like old and dying prisoners huddled at assembly. Their lantern and candlelit windows flickered off into the darkness like hopeless eyes or fading embers of a long-neglected fire. Every few hundred feet, massive stone and rusting metal columns rose into the foreboding shadows to meet the icicles above. Everybody knew what lay beyond, but few knew the details—and then only via secondhand accounts. It was the Empire, as if its very weight seemed to crush down on Donovan's whole world. Compelled by the gravity of it, Donovan scribbled more into the book.

I was born not far from here, in this forgotten hole un'er t'Empire streets. We call it Under City, but 'tis wot's known in t'Empire as "T'Sewers." 'Tis the place where Boss Dog Magistrate hides t'prisons and dumps his trash. 'Tis where he dumped us too, generations ago as legends tell, af'er a great war, as my father accounts.

 They call us "Sewer Rats" and according t'my old man, These Sewers once made up t'original city, t'very seat of t'Empire. 'Tis t'seat, for sure, right un'er Boss Dog's ass.

Just as Donovan scratched out the last period of the last line, a strange moving spotlight appeared far above and a couple blocks over. It probed the darkness with an icy cold blue light, like an alien craft. Donovan knew the light all too well; everybody in the Sewers knew. Its origin was the Colonies, an off-limits part of the Empire—off-limits to "Rats" especially. It was a Colonial Lawbroker patrol. These dangerous two- or four-officer hovercraft rarely ventured from the Colonies to come through the Sewers and when they did so, it was mostly for show. Even though the Lawbrokers had plenty of lethal firepower at their disposal, they never approached close to the Sewer streets unless the population required a public reminder of the deadly face of Imperial power. The Empire preferred to maintain some officious air of false propriety and not soil its hands directly with Sewer issues.

The powers above left that show to the Colonial Constabularies and their boots on the ground, mostly local criminals *pressed into service* to catch or kill runaways like Donovan. They were called the Sewer Guard, a kind of local militia that ran on bribery and fear of punishment from their own masters above. The deal was simple: Be useful or be jailed or be dead. These lost boys and girls were empowered to kill, catch, or torture lawbreaking Rats. The Empire had dangerous eyes indeed.

Donovan had felt the Sewer Guard's brand of state-sponsored discipline before. The Guards carried an electrified livestock prod that doubled as a sort of musket rifle. It was known throughout the Sewers as a Barking Iron and many Rats had died from its bite.

Colonial Lawbrokers only fly down here t'keep us scared and in line. Technically, t'Sewers are property o' t'Empire but those Mules would n'er sully their hands on us. For local law, they use our own kind 'gainst us, t'Sewer Guard. As if there was anythin' o' value down here. Wot better way t'keep t'straight 'n'narrow than t'have your own kind tossed a few extra rocks t'guard the borders, 'n' given e'en bigger rewards fo' killin' runaway knucks like me.

A smart Sewer Guard could make a bounty o' coin in ransom from both family and Empire by holdin' an escaped Rat. Sure, t'Mules got a hefty reward for each kill but most often, they'd do both, take a ransom, then kill t'Rat and pawn off t'poor sod's property to the local "Boxman," or wot we Rats call t'undertaker-pawnbroker.

I been lashed 'n' beaten just fo' eyeballin' a Sewer Guard 'n' felt t'sting of their Barking Irons too. 'Tis that all keeps us in line you might ask? Would were that 'nuff. Boss Dog and his Empire have carefully set up a system o' punishments and rewards. Work harder, obey more rules, serve t'Empire, or be turncoat by yer

7

own family and friends. Do a good job, be a good turncoat, profit t'Empire, maybe, you might win your freedom.

After a few fruitless searches for Rats to scare off, the hovering Colonial Lawbrokers grew bored and moved on. As soon as their unnatural and disembodied light looked elsewhere, Donovan stashed the book in his long waistcoat and bolted for his next stop, a sliver of deep shadow between two badly decrepit tenements.

Regent Street was fairly busy today. Its trash- and debris-strewn cobblestones were populated by Sewer Rats of all ages and ethnicities, going about the grim business of Sewer survival. Wearing a similar range of long waistcoats, hats, and cloaks, they traded scavenged items in dark foreboding sidewalk bazaars that brimmed with damaged and recycled goods. Some better-off Rats with corrupt, black-market Empire connections dealt in more functional technology, along with old canned goods and other purloined supplies that had little use in the Colonies and Empire short of selling off. Despite the energetic activity, though, Sewer Rats barely got what they needed to survive, and the Regent Street markets were little more than second- and third-hand stores, a vast system of trickle-down economics until what trickled was fit for a Sewer.

There were no self-powered vehicles of any kind in the Sewers, only horses and wagons, swine and mules. Whatever rare, familiar-looking parts of the chassis and wheels of once-motorized machines there were to be found were pulled by people and animals alike. Any little bits and bobs of truly usable technology consisted of random and broken pieces and parts of something else. Donovan thought about how it all had such a faraway quality, an affluent feel somehow, but, like the Rats themselves, it was the Empire's trash.

As he ran to his new spot, Donovan struggled to hide the sound of his boots on the greasy and hard cobblestones. He slipped and struggled to time his steps with that of a nearby horse-drawn cart and stuck to the shadows like black paint. Once hidden again, Donovan looked for his next spot. The move would be more trouble. Hanging over the street ahead like some "benevolent" gift was a system of feeble electronic lampposts. These filthy, caged-up, ancient-looking torch lamps struggled to illuminate the dim streets. They gave the entire scene the feel of an eighteenth century London street. It was obvious the Empire cared little about maintaining them, but there was some Imperial technology beyond that they did bother to maintain. On many of the towering support structures, wire-encased, sputtering, and battered flatscreen displays projected the image of a stylized gold crown set against a sea of royal blue; the logo of the Empire. These were the Proclamation Boards, the communication portals of the ruling class. Twenty-four hours a day, they flashed a familiar litany of ever-changing laws, rules, and restrictions, recent arrests, and bizarre offers of hope and encouragement from His "Beneficent" Magistrate William Frederick the Third. There were tiny cameras hidden within the screens as well. More eyes of the Empire.

A particularly bright Proclamation Board made Donovan's next move a little too obvious, so he waited for the moment of darkness as the announcements changed cycles. As the pronouncements paused, Donovan moved locations, but just as he did, the crown on the screen lit up again as if to catch him. He quickly ducked down against a broken wagon and peered back through the splinters of wood and metal. Grabbing at the debris like a crutch, he cut his hand open on a bit of broken glass and drops of Donovan's blood found their way to the street. As he pressed his palm under his arm to stop the flow, the Proclamation Board fired up again and taunted him.

"By order of His Magistrate William Frederick the Third, the following offenses are deemed BLACK FLAG and punishable by time at the lash, indentured servitude, or death: No public assembly of more than six, failure to comply with instructions or orders from Lawbrokers and local Guards, possession of weapons of any kind, sale of Empire-imported goods without paying appropriate tax, any posting of writing of materials or thoughts deemed subversive to the Empire; any attempted escape. Be warned. Be loyal. Serve the Empire and you may win your freedom."

As the flickering light slashed across Donovan's face, the list faded to a propaganda film of an army of teens, both boys and girls, all taken from the streets of Donovan's Under City. Like some kind of magical abduction, they were lifted on a beam of light and transformed into a royal-blue uniformed army. Then, in some futuristic, stylized cityscape, they toiled in the sun, helped children, saved lives, went on to work; they married and raised families in affluence and security. The idyllic scenes were accompanied by an equally hopeful voice.

"Citizens of the Six Lands of the Sewers, look for your chance. Look for the Catchers. BE CHOSEN! Become an Empire Builder. SERVE HIS MAGISTRATE—WIN YOUR FREEDOM!"

The voice pulled at Donovan through a familiar refrain he'd heard since childhood, slipped into story, Imperial message and programmed memories. He'd known Empire Builders before, the fallen ones, the rejects. The official story was that they'd failed selection once inside the Catcher Transport. The rest who left and were seemingly selected never came back. It was like dying and going to an afterlife. There was no real way to prove or disprove any of it, except to be chosen and find out for oneself. As Donovan finished the thought, the display flickered dark as the screen again paused between announcements. Donovan seized the moment of opportunity to move off to a deep shadow under one of the gargantuan Empire supports. Behind him, the crown logo returned as if to watch him go.

At Donovan's next destination, a group of real rats squealed in protest at his arrival. Like any good Empire trained Sewer Rats, this entire nest threatened to give him away until offered a bribe. He reached his still-bleeding hand into the pocket of his long coat and parted with one of his most precious possessions, his Firecake, a simple blend of water, salt, and black-market flour, all baked together by being dropped next to an open fire. Donovan bit off a piece of the stone-hard sustenance. It tasted like smoky wood and was just as hard, but to a fugitive on the run, it tasted of freedom. The teen sighed as he watched the rats eating the rest of his cake. *Everything in the Sewers,* he thought, *involves a deal or payoff.*

My old man croaked in my ninth year. At least t'was what my mum sed. She didn't care much for t'old Black-Flagger, sed he'd run off t'knuck some coin and likely got mustered out or dumped t'rot in t'Constable's Keep.

Af'er he left, I was sent t'live with my older brother Lar to earn a wage. Our mum havin' four more mouths to her brood, couldn't find wage 'nuff t'care for us all. She lived in Ferry Farm, a pleasant 'nuff sounding place, if you fancy living near a giant shite-filled sewage filtration gate.

Lar made some decent rock as a shade farmer down way o' Verne Crossing 'n' we sent what we could back home. I ne'er saw mum much af'er that. Lar also toiled with some dodgy Empire Mule t'make survey maps o' t'Sewers. T'was some handsome coin to be sure, but we both knew why t'Empire would hire a lowly Sewer Rat. Boss Dog wanted Lar to map out all the ways a Rat might escape.

Far as I knew, Lar ne'er finished his maps. He couldn't. He was hiding something 'n' I found out a couple years later when I turned eleven. That's when Lar caught the vapors 'n' died.

B'fore he passed, he gave me some coin 'n' our father's book. Turns out, t'old man was quite taken with making maps too, but his maps were only fo' Rats. Lar kept the secret safe 'nuff but n'er acted on any o'it. Guess he wasn't t'restless type like me. Lar didn't fancy causes. He just wanted t'get his wage and be safe. I always wanted more.

Donovan leaned into shadow just as a passing street vendor peered toward his dark makeshift lair. After the merchant passed, Donovan looked down Regent Street toward several more slivers of light filtering down from high above more of the giant support columns. While it wasn't going to be the most inconspicuous route, that was where he needed to go; column by column and light by light. It was a strange contradiction.

Those light beams were not only bright, they sometimes offered a source of warmth. They also beckoned like portals to the heavens above, but the local Rats knew all too well that their origin wasn't so benign nor hopeful. The light came from nearly a mile above, from the sun as it shined upon the Empire. At certain times of day, clusters of Rats, carefully arranged in groups of three or four so as not to incur Imperial or local discipline, gathered at these spots for a taste of warmth and to ponder what might await them if they got the honor of being chosen as an Empire Builder. Before reading his father's book, Donovan too had looked into the light and wondered. He thought about how the colors he'd always known were so browned, yellowed, and soiled that he could almost smell them. *Brown for shite,* he thought, *gray for rot and filth, and black for death.* On the thought, Donovan was off again, down Regent Street and across an intersection onto a rougher part of the Under City called Auld Way. Perimeter Five was close now—only two streets off—but Auld Way was black-market gang territory and far more dangerous in its own right. That's when the Lawbroker Craft suddenly reappeared and descended from the darkness above, catching Donovan in its blinding spotlight.

"You there, SEWER RAT! Stop and declare your status!" A gruff and authoritative voice thundered from the sleek, hovering craft. Donovan froze. This was the end he had always been taught to expect.

2

PURGATORY

Up close, the sleek Lawbroker machine looked like a combination of a street vehicle and a deadly flying sea creature from some childhood nightmare, with four folded wheels retracted under its wing-like body. While airborne, the vehicle floated on a cushion of glowing magnetic energy which was channeled from eight large metallic underside protrusions nicknamed daisy-roots by Sewer Rats. "Pushin' up daisy-roots" was a common refrain for those who'd been caught by a Lawbroker patrol and subsequently vanished.

Donovan also knew that atop the Lawbroker craft was a powerful net launcher for trapping Rats, a dangerous device that stood alongside two different kinds of far more lethal weaponry. The first was an energy beam of sorts that on low setting was good for what felt like a horrible full-body sunburn. But set on high—what the Lawbrokers called "The Spit"—it cooked a target from the inside out. The second bit of anti-personnel technology looked like an arrow-shooting Gatling gun, only the arrows were paralyzing electrified darts. This bit of ingenious gear was called "The Porcupine."

Donovan watched as the craft descended to within thirty feet of him, so close that the pulsing blue light emanating from the patrol vehicle's sides and crevices washed over and blinded him. The teen was a long way from his mom's in Ferry Farm and was even further from his own home in Dogue Run, Fairfax Flats, meaning he had absolutely no reason to be there. Getting caught by Lawbrokers wasn't the worst thing either. Donovan was dangerously close to Perimeter Five, and, if these Empire policemen found him suspicious enough, they might land and search him. They would then find his father's subversive and Black-Flag book and, in turn, discover Donovan's little revolutionary group hidden in their Dogue Run apartment. The lot of them would certainly be hung for it. Donovan's blood pooled into his core and his body twitched through a rush of adrenaline as the craft hovered to within twenty feet, so close now that the magnetic daisy-roots lifted all the metal on Donovan's clothing and body to weightlessness.

The Lawbroker behind the microphone was already losing his temper. "Declare your status at once or be trapped, tagged, and hauled off to the Constabulary."

The order was simply a taunt. The Lawbroker craft could scan the boy and get his identity anyway. This was a common intimidation tactic used by the Lawbrokers to provoke a telling reaction. Donovan looked up at the glowing craft and tried to put a face to the voice. It was as if Magistrate William Frederick the Third himself was speaking, though Donovan had only seen him depicted by that crown logo. His Magistrate's face was not known to Sewer Rats, so he had no face. He was emptiness; he was like death, a great unknown.

"You already know my status," Donovan yelled back to nobody.

Inside the technology-crammed craft, Lawbroker Lieutenant Silas Tarleton cut an imposing figure in his perfectly arranged gray-blue Colonial Military uniform and silver-white sash. Prematurely gray at twenty-five, Tarleton's long salt-and-pepper mane was slicked back into a ponytail. Even his hair was tight. Tarleton pulled aside his headset microphone and leaned slightly to his left where a young female officer sat.

"Ready the nets, Cruz." The order escaped the side of his mouth as if it was barely an afterthought.

Across from him, Watchman Lee Cruz wasn't nearly as gung-ho about Donovan the Sewer Rat. Compared to Tarleton and his ice-cold demeanor, she was the only human in this machine and, in a sense, it made her an unwilling passenger. Lee Cruz had found her way into the position of Watchman in order to survive. She was born in the northeast Colonies, just outside the inner Empire, and raised in a working-class area, barely a step up from the Sewers except for its meager creature comforts, commercial distractions, and, of course, sunlight. She had something in common with the Sewer Rats and it was likely by design, too, that she'd been paired with the Imperial-born Tarleton. She was there for appearances' sake; she was a calming influence, perhaps—good public relations.

In her close-up camera feed, Cruz's warm eyes met Donovan's wide stare of terror. He looked like a little boy to her and it touched something deep inside. Her mental flip-book flashed to dark and foggy images of a car chase through the streets of Rhodes Colony. The images culminated in a crash to blackness.

"He's just a frightened kid," she unwittingly dismissed her superior. "Why don't we just scan him and move on?"

Tarleton turned away from his monitors and frowned at his junior officer. He looked down at her and, for effect, took note of the total lack of military decoration on her uniform. "You see, Cruz?" he snarled. "That's your problem. Where you mistake innocence, I see corruption in the offing. You don't know these rodents like I do." He turned back to his displays where Donovan was just a target. "We are talking about a common Sewer, after all. They're all guilty of something down in this filth."

"Maybe we all are, Lieutenant…even above." The words entered the craft like a jailbreak from the distance of her mind.

Tarleton's eyes iced over. "Don't push your luck," he hissed. "Constable Gage already has you in his crosshairs; you're one bad report away from the lash."

"I'd rather go back to the Colonies anyway," she fished. "This assignment is a dead end."

Tarleton brushed off the comment by locking the machine's weapons system on Donovan and swooping the craft to within ten feet of him. Still, Tarleton couldn't let the disrespecting words hang. "A hive of bribes and black-marketeering?" he rolled his eyes at her. "Keep talking like that and you'll get yet another assignment—to the blasted KEEP!"

While the lash would only be insult added to injury in her mind, the idea of being sent to the Under City prison that sat on the lower outskirts of the Sewers frightened Cruz. It was a leftover from a more primitive time, built of ancient stone and brick, almost medieval in both design and reputation. Cruz thought again about the accident. Ever since that day, her Empire superiors had held the threat of it over her head. It affected her reasoning and she looked for two escapes now, one for her and one for Donovan. She found both as a motion-detector monitor switched over to a group of boisterous teens turning a corner onto Auld Way. As a possible black market gang, and brazenly over the assembly restrictions by numbering eight, these boys had to be bigger fish. She needed to stall, so she engaged Tarleton as best she could.

"Why don't we set down and question him instead of the nets?" Cruz kept focused on Donovan's eyes.

"In this area?" Tarleton bristled. "Too risky."

"Why?"

"Sewer Guard's built a fairly significant militia down here. While most of them would gladly hang the knuck for us and collect the coin, there are subversives in these shadows. Few friends of the Empire."

Cruz was fascinated that Tarleton would actually be wary of something behind his bluster and uniform of commendations and medals. Each had been bestowed for arrests and kills. The image of Tarleton was suddenly strange to her, especially as her eyes wandered to the door behind him, where still more battle decorations hung. These were painted icons, arranged like the boastful wins of a fighter pilot, a dozen silhouetted Rat decals for runaway kills. Even if just for a moment, Cruz sensed the human hiding behind Tarleton's frigid veneer. He was afraid of something, too. It made her curious about why he'd speak of subversives. "What do you know of it?" She pulled his eyes to hers.

"Not all the Six Lands are loyal, Cruz," Tarleton groused with a condescending tone. "While some are as loyal as Empire Guards—take the PortsCalling Militia to the north, for one—others are in it for themselves, cockroaches and parasitical profiteers like the KnoxTown Tribes and HillsLand Boys in the south. Still others," he began waxing like a professor on the subject, "like Alexandria's Army in the Midlands, think they're a government unto themselves."

"And these subversives?" she asked as she watched Donovan still frozen in the light.

"Been talk of rebellion for years here in Fairfax," he bristled. "Mostly minor and petty acts of defiance, but that's how it starts."

Cruz blinked. "How do you know so much about it?"

"Cut my teeth as an undercover Mule down here." Tarleton sat back with a cocky smirk as he locked the nets and porcupine on Donovan Rush. His confidence restored, he leaned to the craft PA and said, "Hold still, lad. This won't hurt much."

Tarleton then locked eyes with Cruz. "I know where all the bones are buried and who dug the holes. Gonna be a war down here someday." His eyes iced over, but to Cruz, his tone betrayed a sliver of doubt. "Mark my words. Then, we can wipe the lot of them out for good."

"What about them?" Cruz saw her opening and tapped the screen for Tarleton to draw his attention to the group of likely gang members.

"Here now? Who?" he hissed even before looking over. Then, he saw the larger haul. His eyes lit up.

Cruz shifted the spotlight from Donovan to the teens. "Could be a Black-Flag gang. Already illegal assembly. More coin for that lot, I'd wager."

Tarleton frowned but spun the craft towards the group anyway. It would certainly look better on the daily ledger if those boys ran or resisted—would look better on his decal wall, too. He pulled the microphone back to his face. "No assembly! Groups of six maximum! Step forward and declare status!"

In the target monitor, the teens scattered to the side, but a couple of them, out of fear of the light, either because they were actually guilty of something or just guilty of being Rats, took off.

Lieutenant Tarleton smiled. "Here we go…let's hold 'em for the Militia Guard."

Donovan watched as the sleek Lawbroker craft suddenly pulled away from him and fired its nets into the darkness. Instead of running, he lingered on the sight just long enough to take note of the glowing crown logo on the vehicle's back. Then, he turned and dashed off into the nearby ruins. Behind him, the cold spotlight found the nets and the two teens they contained. The boys were pinned down on the cobblestones. The Porcupines fired next, and the helpless Sewer Rats screamed out as arcs of electricity surrounded their bodies. If not for pure chance, Donovan knew it would have been him. He never looked back again after that and quickly followed his father's map into the fringes of Perimeter Five.

There, he found an electrified razor-wire fence adorned with small motion-activated video screens. The fence, too, was on the map, but small arrows indicated that there was a path through it.

"SECTOR FIVE SEWER LIMITS" the flat-screens flashed to life and taunted him. "THIS AREA IS BLACK FLAG! LAWBROKERS HAVE BEEN ALERTED. TURN BACK NOW!"

A red scanning beam then shot out from under the screen closest to Donovan and ran over Donovan's body and face, tracing his shape and vitals. Donovan knew this, too, from his father's book, a necessary evil. He was being *measured*, an old Imperial term for being catalogued and recorded. He didn't care. With any luck, in a few minutes, he'd be little more than an Empire mystery, a forgotten Rat.

He quickly retreated back into shadow and snuck to the side towards a nearly collapsed arch that had also been noted on his father's map. As Donovan approached the indicated spot, every Empire warning sign within sight lit up. "THIS AREA UNDER WATCH—IT IS BLACK FLAG—DONOVAN WASHINGTON RUSH—FARFAX FLATS—DOGUE RUN. YOU HAVE

BEEN MEASURED—GO BACK AT ONCE—TRESPASS-ING MEANS DEATH!" Donovan crept up to the collapsed arch and bent down. Within the broken stones was a small space cut into the fence and then carefully rewired around it so that the electronics would think the barrier still whole. *The old man was even better with the black arts than I knew.* The teen smiled inwardly and squeezed into the cramped threshold and through.

Donovan then climbed to his feet inside of the forbidden Perimeter Five. The small arch had opened up on a cavernous dark space. Gone were the massive support columns that punctured the Sewer like the sharp sticks of a ditch-styled trap. Gone were the ancient-looking brownstones and narrow wooden tenements. They were replaced by large and even more ancient stone structures and parapets, all collapsed and crushed down. They looked like war ruins, and the entire place was deserted outside of vermin and pests. At the sight, Donovan took a moment to add to his father's journal.

When I b'gan to read my father's book, I thought t'old man e'en more beetle-headed than my mum said. But as I b'gan to read more 'n' follow his maps, I learned t'truth of it. My old man didn't run out. He'd set out t'reach the Empire. Not in t'usual 'n' Boss Dog accepted way as a blasted Empire Builder, but in t'illegal and Black-Flag way, by breaking out of t'Sewers and leaving a trail that only a bunch of thievin' knucks could follow. A thievin' knuck like me.

21

My old man wasn't just a runaway, wasn't some simple knuck lookin' fo' some easy rock, t'was a God's honest revolutionary.

For t'past six years, I carefully sought out my kind and kin on Dogue Run, Fairfax Flats. Rats like me, tired o' this life, tired o' t'Empire's rules 'n' regulations, willin' t'die for freedom. F'years, we stayed in t'shadows of our own dark world, plannin' our moves. Me and my Brothers and Sisters of the Sword. Johnay, Abi, Crispus, Tommy, Carr, Payne, and Grey are all in with me.

We used t'words in this book t'rise up in Fairfax, take on Boss Dog's local Sewer Guard 'n' gain our own place in Dogue Run. 'Tis time fo' more. Freedom or death 'tis our creed.

I haven't told them what t'was I'd planned today, Johnay especially woulda tried 'n' stop me. I had to see if my old man was right, if there truly was a way out of these stinkin' Sewers.

Lucky fo' me, the book included an entire guide to t'black arts, how t'make fire rocks, smokies, and boom traps. T'old man also wrote about how t'break into things, and how t'break out. Today, I got a mind for both. T'day, I put myself 'n' t'words to t'test. May t'Almighty protect me in my quest.

After dotting the once-empty page with a final period, Donovan leaned back against a broken stone wall. Despite its jagged surface, it felt strangely comforting, finally a part of his world beyond the Sewer. Donovan took a few somber breaths. He knew the journey had only just begun.

Donovan turned his attention back to his father's maps and followed the directions toward an endless maze of debris and broken foundations. There, he reached a spot where the ruins piled high into and against an immense earthen and rocky mound. It was so large that the sides and top of it vanished into darkness. The ruins of a vast castle-fort littered the mound, it too going on and on into the darkness above and beyond. According to the map, unbelievably, this was where the Sewers ended. Donovan froze both on the sights and the implications. All his life, he'd been taught that the Sewers were endless. His father's book said otherwise. Now, Donovan knew for himself.

The teen knelt down, pulled off his backpack, and retrieved a tarnished oil lamp and a crude pickax from inside. He fired up the flickering lamp and again checked his father's book. The castle ruin was marked with arrows and notes along with the hopeful label, "The way." Another arrow connected the phrase across the book gutter to the next page where another cutaway map indicated there was a tunnel inside of that very hill and castle fortress, the entrance of which was marked with the same phrase on the book's cover: *Libertatem*. All Donovan had to do was to find that statue.

Donovan skulked past broken walls and buttresses until he found what he was looking for. Just as the drawing said, the statue's head, arms, and torso had all been long-since looted, but what remained were the legs, one broken at the knee and the other just above the ankle. On the stone pedestal was the word *Libertatem*, just as his father had noted. Donovan's heart raced as he hovered over the stone. His father had been here right on this very spot. His story was real, and the old man was right!

Donovan had already used his father's words to help inspire and band his group of disenfranchised teens together. He'd even cautiously spread the words through other trusted friends and even into remote parts of the Sewers, but this was a whole new chapter. He'd used the words and maps to catch the restlessness of their spirit and lift it like wings on a mighty breeze. But while his self-described "Brothers and Sisters of the Sword" talked about changing the world, actually doing so was another matter. The Empire was a powerful military machine that could defeat any enemy and a staggering economic giant that could win wars without firing a shot, but, most of all, it controlled the narrative and the approved history. The Empire owned the mind. Long ago, Donovan decided this adventure was not just for him, but for his extended family and for all the Sewer Rats, to prove that there was substance behind his father's words, power behind his belief in them, and freedom at the end of a truly independent thought. Even if it meant death.

Still, alone and so far from Dogue Run and well past the point of no return, doubt crept into Donovan's mind, doubt about the book and the words. Might this be as far as his father got? Somehow the very doubt connected father and son, as surely the elder Rush had wrestled with the very same demons of doubt when he made his maps and wrote of freedom. Donovan suddenly felt like he wasn't alone, and as he knelt down to brush the dirt and debris away from the letters on the pedestal, two large shapes rose behind him. Donovan bit down on his lip as the shadows crossed his sightline. He'd been found by a couple of wayward teens from the menacing Fairfax Sewer Guard, and they knew they had this Rat dead to rights.

"Here now," a low voice growled. "Looks like this little Rat has jumped t'maze."

Donovan couldn't even turn before the larger of the two kicked him forward onto the pedestal. Donovan's head glanced off the edge, cutting open his brow. He reflexively looked back at the immediate threat and brought his hand to the wound. He was bleeding badly and, for a moment, his anger brushed away his fear and he glared up at his two assailants.

The Sewer Guards were dressed like Donovan but instead of tricorne hats, they wore stylized, three-pointed helmets and midnight-blue waistcoats, their little Empire-provided badges of dishonor. On their left arms, they also wore blue armbands with the Empire gold crown emblazoned on them—and on the bands were pinned small commendations for Rat traps or kills. These weren't just Militia Rats; these were decorated Sewer Guards.

The smaller of the two extended his Barking Iron, its tip ominously flickering with electricity before being driven into Donovan's chest. The released shock fired every nerve in the teen's body and his back arched so hard the bones in his spine almost cracked. Spit and tears erupted from Donovan's shaking face as his brain went haywire. He could barely contain his bodily fluids as he spasmed. In a second, the guard withdrew the Iron and waited as Donovan's twitches subsided.

Then he smiled to his partner. "Soon as he's done soilin' himself, let's see if he's got any cheese on him."

Then, with a flick of the wrist, both guards telescoped their Barking Irons into their even more deadly mode, that of long rifle-like devices. They trained them on Donovan. One shot from these would kill.

"By order of His Magistrate, William Frederick t'Third," the larger guard growled, "this place 'tis Black Flag. Bein' caught here means death…" The guard waited a beat for effect. "D'you have any final words 'fore we carry out sentence?"

Dazed and hurt, Donovan looked up at them as he reached into his pocket.

"Here now," the shorter guard cautioned. "Don't be doin' nuthin' immediately suicidal."

Donovan's mouth opened but nothing came out.

The smaller guard smiled cruelly. "Give it a moment, y'can speak soon," his eyes flashed darkly. "If'n we let ya."

"I got a lotta coin…on me 'n' at home…" Donovan rasped weakly as he tried to bargain. "If you let me go…"

The larger teen cut him off with a laugh. "Ya stupid Knuck. We can shoot you, empty y'pockets, and still get y'coin as reward!"

Donovan waited a beat and shook his head knowingly. "Fairfax Militia Boys," he hissed.

He got another quick shock for his defiance. "What of it?" the larger guard taunted.

Donovan's voice quaked through the electrical aftershock. "In it fo' no cause but rock."

"'N' you stand fo' what?" One of them folded his arms.

"Freedom."

The two looked at each other. Fine words that in this reality meant nothing more than quaint hyperbole. They both laughed.

"Fair 'nuff. Maybe, if'n y'tell us how 'tis you came by here?" the larger guard reasoned, suddenly thinking of a possible bigger reward. "We might b'inclined t'let you purchase some o' said freedom," he began to cackle. "Long 'nuff t'live t'see t'Keep."

Slowly, Donovan pulled his hand from his pocket and then fired a small, tightly bundled ball into the ground.

"See THIS!" Donovan shouted as the small ball exploded with a bright flash of fire and sparks. The two guards yelped like

26

startled dogs and then fired their barking Irons into the growing column of thick, acrid, black smoke. It temporarily burned their eyes, leaving them little recourse but to frantically wave at nothing for several seconds. Once their vision and the smoke cleared, they choked and waded forward but found nothing. Donovan was gone somehow.

The larger Sewer guard turned a frightened face to his partner. "Blast it!" He put his head on a swivel. "Look for Boss Dog's cameras…. If Lawbrokers saw us screwin' up, we'll be jobbed off to t'Boxman!

"He couldn't have gone far," the smaller guard assured, not believing his own words.

The Sewer guards quickly moved off, leaving the statue pedestal behind. They didn't realize that it was shifted to the side imperceptibly and that there was a tiny sliver of light growing from a crack under it. In their haste and fear, the guards also didn't notice that Donovan had left a bloody handprint on the side of the pedestal; it looked strangely like the hand holding the star from the cover of his father's book. The Sewer guards quickly spread out and moved off to search the ruins.

Donovan waited under the pedestal until the guards were out of sight. Then, he turned his small oil lamp back to full brightness and found the opening to a long, underground tunnel spreading out before him. The rocky passage led off into the darkness and, as near as Donovan could tell from the map, directly under the great earthen mound, just as the book had foretold.

For the next several minutes, his desperate hands and boots pried at the cold rock and dirt in search of traction and handholds. He hung his small lantern from his chest, causing his moving limbs to send long and eerie shadows in every direction.

Suddenly, it looked like every Rat in the Sewer was there with him in shadow.

After ten minutes of clambering, Donovan found an ante-chamber of sorts where he dimmed his lantern and waited a couple of minutes in the darkness and listened for sounds. Nothing. He was safe for now. Both he and his father's book.

Donovan took a sip of water from a small canteen and chewed through a few bites of his last remaining Firecake. He smiled. The progress toward his goal seemed to make it taste better somehow. Donovan paused to think about how far he'd really come. It was only a few miles of Sewer, but now he'd also traveled across worlds. In the eyes of the law, he'd passed the threshold of death as well. Donovan opened to the very first page of his father's notes, the first words that had caught his eye six years before, just in his eleventh year of life, the words that began this journey—words that inspired him still.

Society in every state is a blessing, but Government, even in its best state, is but a necessary evil; in its worst state, an intolerable one. For when we suffer or are exposed to the same miseries by a government, which we might expect in a country without government, our calamity is heightened by reflecting that we furnish the means by which we suffer. Government, like dress, is the badge of lost innocence; the palaces of kings are built upon the ruins of the bowers of paradise. For were the impulses of conscience clear, uniform, and irresistibly obeyed, we would need no other lawgiver. But that not being the case, we find it necessary to surrender up a part of our property to furnish means for the protection of the rest, and this we are induced to do by the same prudence which in every other case advises us, out of two evils, to choose the least. Wherefore, security being the true design and end of government, it unanswerably follows that whatever form thereof appears most likely to ensure it to us, with the least expense and greatest benefit, is preferable to all others.

Since then, Donovan often wondered why there was an Empire at all, why there were Rats and why the Empire Lawbrokers kept such a close watch on them. Fellow Rats to Donovan looked just like Lawbrokers only without the fancy uniforms and technology. It didn't seem to be about race or about allegiances. Were the Rats really victims of a past war as his father had written? Why was the world this way? How did it get so inequitable and unfair? Was the Empire simply the lesser of two evils as his father had written about, or had it moved far beyond that seemingly quaint notion and, like Donovan, into wholly uncharted territory? Then, there was the most important question of all: What was awaiting him at the end of his father's words? The last question brought Donovan back to the moment. He couldn't turn back now, even if he'd wanted to. If Dr. Rush was right, the teen reasoned that his choice was not the lesser of evils but rather, the measure of opportunity and dreams. At least, that's what he told himself as he plowed ahead into the unknown. Ahead, there was a single, narrow passageway, framed with stones to reinforce it. It looked like a doorway, but to what? The gravity of it all nagged and pulled at Donovan, almost pulling him down. But it was the thought of all the work his father had put into his book—not for himself but for others, for future sons and daughters—that pulled Donovan forward.

Death's just a doorway. That's what I 'member my ol' man tellin' me 'fore he left fo' good. Dyin' he said, t'was merely an exit from all things we know of, 'tis all. Freedom from life he'd say...but true Freedom, he said, begins with a single free thought.

This book, 'tis full o' thoughts. Fragments o' my father's story. 'Tis chock fulla ramblings on life, freedom, and t'all-powerful Empire that long ago, he said, took e'rything away from the Sewers and t'Colonies too. Truth be told, what my father truly left me, t'was somethin' far better than words. He left me somethin' t'believe in...and for now, t'was more than 'nuff to go on.

With his and his father's cause now joined somewhere between the Sewers and the Empire, Donovan took the next step and passed the stony threshold. Ahead in the darkness, he found a larger open cave where his feeble lantern light revealed a moving maze of long shadows and multiple pathways. The long shadows, in turn, revealed dozens of stalactites and cracks in the flat, low ceiling above. Water dripped down from there; slivers of light followed. There were cave-ins on two sides that blocked two possible passages, and Donovan quickly assessed that this might not be the safest place to dawdle. Then, he saw it. Crudely chiseled into the rock above him and near where the water dripped down was the hand holding the star icon. The pathway out was up. Pressing into the cracked ceiling, he found that it wasn't stone at all, but instead was loose cement and dirt. It was a signpost.

Donovan reached into his shoulder pack and pulled out his crude pickax and tapped it into the surface. A few more drops of water rained down from it, along with some small rocky rubble. He swung again and a gush of water rushed out like the cavern above was about to give birth. The water hit him hard and he slid back in a panic, expecting to drown. Then, a huge chunk of the ceiling gave way and was about to crush him until the teen managed to roll aside at the last moment. As Donovan caught his breath, the water flow abated, and revealed light coming from a human-sized hole above. Cautiously, Donovan approached the opening and tried to look up; there were more stones up there, not a natural formation, but hand-laid masonry.

"SHITE!" Donovan tried and failed to muffle the amazement in his voice. Had he found the lower levels of the Empire?

3

RESURRECTION

As DONOVAN PULLED HIMSELF UP, the first thing he noticed was the large rusted metal pipe leaking from high above. It was nestled between two sickly-yellow sulfur lights. Donovan guessed he'd hit an Empire maintenance tunnel, so he pulled himself up into the dark space to get a better look. There, he sat back to catch his breath and assess the moment. As he spun his lamp around, Donovan found himself surrounded by stone walls on two sides and by badly rusted iron bars on the other two. He had broken into a jail cell—a wet and leaky jail cell at that.

An ominous and scratchy cackle bled into the scene from across the darkened hall and Donovan crept forward towards it. As he got close to the bars of his strange cell, he was able to focus across the hall to another set of bars. Behind those were another cell, where a wild-eyed old man looked back with a dirty and gap-toothed smirk.

"Outta one blasted cage and into the next, eh, lad?" the old man cackled again.

Donovan could only blink.

"What's the matter, son?" The old man's eyes flashed a more pointed look. "Boss Dog got your tongue?" He cackled again.

"Where is this place?"

The old man stood up into the light. He was wearing the soiled and tattered clothing of a Sewer Rat; his long white hair and beard made it seem like he'd been in prison forever.

Donovan was confused by the sight. While the tattered old man looked like just another Sewer Rat, he spoke like a Lawbroker.

"All this hump just to break into the Constable's Keep...." The old man let out a deep, heaving sigh. "'Tis a damn shame, eh?"

Donovan tried to ignore him and his sudden empathy. The teen had gotten this far on his own; certainly his empty cell wasn't locked.

"Not fo' long," Donovan grumbled as he brushed himself off and tried the door. It was indeed locked. The old man just stared at him now. No more laughing. He looked concerned.

Donovan glared back at him, then casually reached into his backpack and pulled out a set of ancient-looking lockpicks.

"I got bigger plans, ol' man...." Donovan's glare softened into a smirk as he went to work on the lock.

"Trained in the black arts, I see." The old man pulled himself close to the bars of his cell to study Donovan closer. His eyes narrowed. "Exactly what is your business here, knuck?"

Donovan ignored him as he struggled with the lock.

"No matter which way you go lad, you'll never get out...." He pressed the teen. "But I know the true way!"

Donovan stopped. "Wot d'you know? Stuck in there rottin' like a dead fish?"

"Empire's a jail just like any other, son" the old man offered. "I'm free...no matter where they keep me." He tapped at his temples.

Quite sure the old man's mind was gone, Donovan went back to work. "I b'lieve different…." he muttered as he struggled anew with the lock.

"How's that?" the crazy-eyed prisoner challenged.

Donovan worked a few moments more and the lock finally yielded. Donovan eyed the old man as he swung the door open with a defiant smile. "Freedom or death, sir," Donovan said as he stepped out into the hall.

The old man's eyes suddenly went wide. He pulled back from the bars and it plunged his face back into ominous shadow. "Here now, boy," he stammered. "Where'd you hear such words?" His voice was strangely shaken.

Donovan stopped mid-step. Something was off. He stared into the cell and locked eyes with the old prisoner. "From my father…." Donovan half-whispered before raising his voice back up. "Wot's it to you?"

The old man staggered back to the bars and grabbed onto them this time as if he needed them for support. "Your father?" the old man stammered again. "Your…father…"

His own words stopped his mind cold until a new idea thawed something deep within.

"Who was your father?" the man suddenly rasped.

Donovan blinked again, before looking down. "I barely knew him." His voice went distant as he reached into his pack and held up the book. "I only know him from his words."

The old man gave the book a strange look, but distracted by other concerns, Donovan turned to look for an exit. "Ok, ol' man. Which way is t'way out?"

"What you really seek, I believe…" the old man eyed him deeper "…is a way in."

Donovan blinked again as a sparkle slowly formed in the old man's eyes. "What you really need to decide, lad, is which one 'tis the lesser of two evils."

Donovan lost his breath. Those were his father's words. Before Donovan could respond, the old man looked the teen over again, slowly, and up and down. As he tilted his head forward, his long, white hair flopped across his face. When he pulled it back, there were the beginnings of tears in his eyes.

"You've grown so much…."

Donovan spun back as his mouth fell open.

"My Donnie boy." Dr. Rush's voice cracked.

Donovan tried to utter the obvious "Father?" but not a sound came from his mouth.

Dr. Rush heard the word regardless, as two separate tears coalesced and streaked down his face. "You followed my trail of crumbs," he choked out the words. "You grew up just as I thought." He beamed proudly now. "Just as I'd hoped!"

Donovan's expression faded to uncertainty.

"The map led here?" he suddenly gasped. "'Tis as far as you got?"

"Much further lad, but this t'was as far as I dared reveal," his father tried to guide him. Dr. Rush firmly grabbed onto the bars of his cell. "The only way in. A way back."

"I don't understand," Donovan finally muttered. "The way in t'wot? The way back?" he paused. "T'wot?"

"I used to live in the Empire my boy, until they cast me out."

It took Donovan a few moments to process it, at once confusing and incendiary. "You sayin' I'm son t'all I hate 'n' fight 'gainst?" Donovan bit down hard on his thoughts. He regretted the words the moment they left his lips.

"I had two evils, Donnie." Rush sternly looked back. "Death or the Keep." The father tried to focus his boy. "They tossed me here when I began preaching 'bout liberty, but I broke out t'get that book t'Lars 'n' you. To leave you the trail."

"Why didn't Boss Dog just pack you off to t'Boxman?"

"They couldn't kill me, Donnie." Dr. Rush was as brazen as a man could be behind bars. "I've still a few friends in t'Empire, lad; they protected me and what I know."

"Why?"

"Gonna have t'ask them now, won't cha?" Rush's eyes sparkled a hopeful challenge.

Donovan ran his hands over the journal. Surely this book wasn't as important as that. "They wanted this?"

Dr. Rush nodded as he watched the avalanche of thought and emotion pooling behind his son's eyes. "Aye. The way in, Donnie," Rush tugged at his bars. "'Tis the way back."

Donovan was frozen. He could only mumble, "Through the Keep?" He huffed. "'Nuff puzzles...."

Dr. Rush nodded. "The other way in is through the filtration gates beyond Ferry Farm, 'n' from there, out into the Channel." He pushed his face close to the bars. "To the colonies!"

"T'filtration gates are guarded by whole Regiments o' Fairfax Militia," Donovan sighed incredulously. "'Tis no way past 'em."

Dr. Rush's eyes opened wide again and he looked to the ceiling as if for divine inspiration. "Up above the Fairfax Flats area, high atop t'spires, past the wires and cameras, are catwalks t'Empire Mules use for maintenance."

Donovan tried to think. "But 'tis surely watched! Boss Dog must have it un'er lock 'n'key."

"You think all those cameras still work? You think the Empire Mules can watch them all?" Rush's voice lowered into a pointed mix of plea and disdain. "That's how they win, lad, they get you t'catch yourselves. They defeat yer minds long before they defeat yer cause. Owning t'land and yer money and work is an easy thing. Once you own t'people's will, you own it all."

Rush's brows arched. "Lesser of two evils, my boy."

Dr. Rush then reached out his rough and gnarled hands. "Pass me the book and your implement," he beckoned. "Quickly."

Donovan slipped the volume through the bars and handed his father his quill. Rush began to scribble a new map just after where his boy had stopped writing. It was a diagram of an immense river called The Channel, and where it touched the Fairfax filtration gates, and where the Colonies were in relation. Rush then marked the closest colony, *Rhodes*.

Donovan stood transfixed as his father sketched the waterfront and beach and labeled it *New Town*. He then marked the Lawbroker stations, work areas, docks, warehouses, and streets beyond all the way to another spot labeled *Prudence Town*. "Here's the waterfront of NewTown in Rhodes, lad," Rush directed as he sketched. "Here are the sentry points, the best way 'cross Thames Street and though the warehouses. Prudence Town is twenty miles north. Go there to a pub called the Red Fez on Peck Street."

"Red Fez?" Donovan wondered aloud.

"Black market haunt," Dr. Rush smiled. "Good place to slake your thirst and hide after such a long and Black-Flag journey."

Donovan's father than marked the Fez with a deep *X*. He then looked up with a smile and passed the book back through the bars. "T'will be a well-earned reward."

Donovan studied the book and the drawings until another thought bubbled up. "You said 'tis t'way in?"

Dr. Rush nodded.

"Wot, then, 'tis t'way back?"

"That, my boy," Rush smiled. "Is what the book and this grand experiment was all about!"

Donovan reached for his lockpicks. "You're coming with me."

Rush reached through the bars and grabbed his boy's hands. "NO!" His eyes darted down the long, stone corridor. "Not now!"

"Wot are you talkin' about?" Donovan protested. "Why not?"

"I said not now!" Rush looked off down the long hall and lowered his voice to a wary rasp. "It's better they find me here. 'Tis where I'm not a threat. Get to Rhodes Colony boy…get to the Fez!"

Donovan followed his father's gaze to far down the tunnel, where the swinging lights of electronic LED lanterns flickered like an approaching blue fire. They were accompanied by the dangerous sound of thumping boots, clanging keys, and rustling body armor.

"It's the Guard of the Keep!" Rush's eyes blazed in the light from the dim yellow torches above. "You came for freedom…but that'd be certain death!" Rush pressed his face to the bars. "Run, boy! RUN!"

The Keep guards got close enough to spot movement. One of them called out. "Here now, who's lurking about down there? Declare yourself!"

The command caused Donovan's spine to involuntarily straighten. He also reflexively looked down the hall just enough to see the shape of the two guards emerging into the light. They didn't look like Sewer Militia, either; they were in full flack gear and helmets. Donovan saw the outlines of their far bigger weapons. These men weren't like the wayward teens he knew; they were Imperial soldiers.

Donovan rushed back into his cell and leapt down into the hole. Before he vanished completely, he stopped and looked back at his father. "I'll be back for you."

Before the teen could duck down out of sight, Rush called out. "Remember Donnie, freedom ain't given…it's taken…by them or by you…." His face became dark and determined. "TAKE IT, DONNIE! TAKE IT!"

Down the hall, the Keep guards broke into a run. "WHO'S DOWN THERE?!?"

Donovan slipped on the edge of the hole and fell in. He landed hard in the mud and water and lost his breath. Above him, the guards rushed into the cell and shined their focused, blue LED torches down towards him. Donovan watched the two hulking shadows hover above as he moved back and forth to avoid the focused lights. His lungs and back ached from the fall and he gasped for breath. Any second, they'd be upon him.

"STOP! WHOEVER YOU ARE!" the guards thundered.

From their own vantage point, the two guards could only see glimpses of Donovan's shadow and the dirt and water that moved from his body squirming just out of sight. The elder Rush watched in fear as the larger of the guards prepared to jump down.

"Sound the alarm," he bellowed to his partner before diving into the hole.

Donovan managed to scurry back towards the antechamber as the hulking Keep guard followed.

Above in the Keep, the other guard paused to look at Rush before bolting into the hall and toward a decrepit old alarm box.

"You there! You spoke with the knuck?" the guard demanded.

Dr. Rush just shrugged.

"Answer me or I'll muster you out on my own authority, no matter who up there minds you!"

Rush just shrugged and smiled as the guard pulled the alarm. He knew he was in little danger. The Empire sent him here to rot and the less the guards knew about him the better. Best they not ask him any questions about what he knew, lest they implicate themselves. The Empire's tactics of fear and control lived beyond the Sewers. As the guard quickly moved on and the alarm sounded, the entire facility echoed with a horrible electronic scream. The guard then went to the hole and jumped in to join in the pursuit.

Down in the tunnels, Donovan turned this way and that. Wherever he looked, it was a dead end. He'd lost his bearings. Partly frozen with questions and fear about the fate of his father, Donovan chose the only tunnel he could find and rolled into it. He hit a sudden drop and fell crashing down. It was a dead end, a drain of sorts, with a huge, grated wall blocking the only possible exit. As the teen turned back, the first, more hulking Keep guard rose into his path. The boy quickly reached into his coat and fired off one of his homemade smoke bombs, but it was wet and useless. Silently, the large Keep guard smiled and raised his weapon, a far deadlier looking Barking Iron than the antiquated models that had found their way into the Sewers.

"Hold fast, little Rat," the guard hissed. "Or I'll muster you out as sure as you stand before me."

With no other way out but through his adversary, Donovan tried a desperate move and hurled himself against the large grating behind him. The rocky structure surrounding the grate began to crack and, emboldened by it, Donovan hurled himself again. The large Keep guard responded by jabbing the Barking Iron into Donovan's back. The teen instantly crumpled in agony, wrapped in the clutches of the device's blue lighting. His nerve pathways overwhelmed, every muscle in Donovan's body went dead. His mind jumbled into a peculiarly mindless state of life and death alertness. He thought about dying and yet didn't seem to care.

With Donovan quivering on the ground, the Keep guard calmly stood over him and raised a wrist radio to his face.

"Got a runaway below block D. Caught the blasted knuck tryin' to break in. Can ya' imagine it?"

The response on the radio was loud enough for the still-paralyzed Donovan to hear. "That's a new one…." the voice nearly chuckled.

"Permission to liquidate?" The guard asked. "Violation of Magistrate Order 76-4-7…."

In the next precious moments, Donovan regained enough movement to turn his head and look up. He watched helplessly as the Keep guard twisted the dial on his Barking Iron and approached. The Iron responded by telescoping into a much deadlier-looking device.

"It'll be over in a second, lad. I'll make it quick."

Donovan felt a tingling in his limbs as his nerves began to reawaken. Slowly, some movement returned, and something jabbed into his side. Pressed under his body when he fell was his own backpack and, inside of it, was the pickax. Just as the guard's fingers twitched at the trigger of the Iron, Donovan pulled the pickax from his backpack and drove it into the guard's foot. The pick end went clean through to the dirt below and the guard fell back, his foot still nailed to the ground for a sickening moment until it agonizingly pulled free and the guard let out a bloodcurdling scream and the Barking Iron tumbled away.

Still trying to shake off the electrical shock, Donovan staggered to his feet and stumbled as if drunk and drugged. He managed to grab the Barking Iron, but clumsy fingers and lack of knowledge combined to form ten full seconds of complete and useless confusion during which the guard recovered enough to slam the Iron away with his good foot. A second later, the huge soldier was up again and driving a rock-like fist into Donovan's face.

"You dandy little prat," he raged. "I'm gonna muster you out with my bare knuckles."

The world spun on its axis as Donovan hit the tunnel wall. Between the massive blow and the electrical shock, Donovan was out on his feet. He stumbled this way and that like a marionette and then tumbled to his knees. His head slumped down and his world grew dark and cold. The second guard entered the tunnel behind and stopped at the sight.

"Looks like I missed all the merriment," he mock-complained.

"I dunno," the larger guard chortled as he sparked his Iron a few times. "I think you can take in a few more shots at him."

As the two shared a sickly laugh, Donovan's strength returned via rage, and he managed, in one sudden burst, to leap up and charge them. The sight of the leaping teen screaming out a battle cry took both guards by surprise and Donovan managed to knock the smaller of the two off his feet, but the larger man was a different story—he caught the lad by the neck and swung him around into an arm-breaking hold. Donovan instantly cried out as his shoulder began to separate. Instead of breaking the lad's arm, though, the large guard put his other huge paw square in the center of Donovan's back and hurled him forward towards the iron grate. Instead of the desired result of Donovan pancaking into the rough rusty bars, the lad's body burst through the rotting metal, and he tumbled away into the darkness beyond.

Far below and after a forty-foot tunnel plunge and five-foot drop straight down, Donovan Washington Rush lay in a pool of hot wastewater. Semiconscious, he took in a few gulps of the noxious brew and began to choke. He reflexively awakened and wretched out the vile and polluted liquid before gasping for oxygen. After a few more painful moments of convulsed hacking, he caught his breath. It felt like a strange rebirth of sorts. As his

eyes came into focus, Donovan realized where he'd landed—
smack into the cobblestones of Auld Way. Not a rebirth, but more
of a near-death experience. Across from him, a crowd of Sewer
Rats gathered and pointed in his direction. Donovan knew why,
and the reason was a clear and present danger to him. If he was a
runaway as they seemed to suspect, his capture was worth a pretty
rock and some other Empire baubles. A moment's hesitation con-
firmed his fear as he heard murmurs from the crowd of "runaway"
and "make us some coin."

Donovan didn't give the crowd time to decide. He leapt up on
woozy legs and scurried off. All that did was embolden a couple
of Rats in the crowd to run to the nearest Empire vid screen and
punch in a citizen's report. Behind the commotion, Donovan
took off down Auld Way and, as he regained his strength, sprinted
onto Regent Street. There, he slowed a bit and tried to blend into
the crowd, but now everything was different.

As he moved past groups of faceless Sewer Rats huddled
around trash fires, he tried to mingle with the hollow-faced, grim
human shadows, but he knew he stuck out. He was no longer
one of them. He was battered, bloodied, and bruised, and the
other Rats seemed to sense the stink on him, like he was carrying
a secret cargo of poison that threatened to bring the whole nest
down. Donovan didn't linger on the sight nor the cold realization.
He broke into a full-on run again and raced for Dogue Run in
Fairfax Flats. It was only a quarter mile away.

As he turned into his own neighborhood, the once-garden spot
of the Old City spread out before him. The streets here opened up
into once-lush squares and parks which now contained only darkened shanty villages and sketchy trader markets. Beyond the main
square rose the familiar and reassuring shape of Donovan's home
base, his four-story group squatters' home. He slowed down and

relaxed, but before he could even set a single boot in the park area that separated him from his sanctuary, Donovan and four other teens next to him were hit with a brilliant white light.

Donovan slumped down to accept his Lawbroker fate, but hovering above him was a far larger craft than the Lawbroker patrol. This one looked more like a tall ship from oceans past—something out of a tattered old painting he'd once seen. The large vessel was bowed out and bloated at the sides, gun emplacements wrapped around it in every direction. Donovan shielded his eyes in the light and swore he could make out men at the rails. Three of the other kids bolted and Donovan watched as they got a mere ten or so steps before they were swallowed up in catch nets. The light stayed on him.

"YOU! RAT! HOLD THERE!" a disembodied voice called from high above. Donovan suddenly knew all too well what was happening as a scanning blue laser traced his form. It was a Catcher—and Donovan Washington Rush was getting what the Empire had taught them was every Rat's wish. He was going to the Empire after all, but he was going as an Empire Builder.

Up at the rails were three Empire guards wearing dark-blue waistcoats and menacing tricorne helmets that covered their faces. Donovan could see they were peering at a view screen as his photo and known information reflected over their shielded eyes.

"DONOVAN WASHINGTON RUSH" was followed by an ID number, "2221732," and an address, "DOGUE RUN 22—FAIRFAX FLATS."

One of the Imperial guards, clearly of higher rank based on his more colorful uniform and sash, turned to his partners. His faceless voice filtered through the speaker in his helmet. "He'll do nicely. Bring him in!"

The stunned Donovan, along with the three other teens, felt their bodies go weightless as a magnetic beam lifted them into the light. Donovan looked down at the confused Rats below; some stared in fear, others applauded. These were the Rats that, as his father said, had bought into the Empire's tale of redemption—they were applauding him being chosen, like he'd won some kind of grand lottery.

As Donovan was lifted higher and higher, he suddenly caught a glimpse of the catwalks his father had told him of. *There was a way out!* Then, the light went out, and with an unceremonious crash, Donovan landed in the belly of the Imperial beast among a sea of other bodies. Before he could stand, he was grabbed by a faceless Imperial guard and tossed aside into a far wall.

"LINE UP!" the guard commanded.

Dull greenish lights came up, revealing a virtual human toilet of a cargo hold. Soiled bodies and the dirty faces of his kind leered back at Donovan in the stinking darkness. The Imperial guards then withdrew behind metal doors and the room lit up in hot white light. The entire mass of people, all consisting of teens and even younger boys, were then hit with water cannons spraying out from hidden nozzles on every wall. After a few painful beats, the water shut down and the side walls of the cargo hold slid open on rows of pristine, royal-blue coveralls, each marked with the stylized crown emblem of the Empire. The Imperial guards returned to prod their catch into their new uniforms.

"Listen up, Rats!" the more decorated of the blank-faced Imperials barked through his speaker in a flat, uninspired, and rehearsed tone. "I am Captain Lepps. Today is your lucky day! Today, we do you a great honor. A chance to serve His Magistrate and perhaps one day…earn your freedom. Today, you become Empire Builders!"

Donovan hesitated getting into the uniform, holding his backpack containing the book and pickaxe close to his chest. One of the Imperial guards approached as small holes opened on the floor, a glowing, orange light and heat emanating from within them.

"All of your filthy personal effects, into the flashers!" Captain Lepps commanded from behind an electrified Barking Iron.

A group of four other Imperials, two dressed like doctors of a sort, entered the hold with a strange device. It looked like a single-bar manacle that had one wrist cuff far larger than the other. Donovan knew about this too—one of his "Brothers of the Blade," Crispus, had the "honor" of being chosen to be an Empire Builder for a few moments before being inexplicably rejected and dumped back onto the street, the fall breaking both his legs. It was a laser tattoo manacle that the Empire used to burn a crown symbol and identification number into the forearm of all Empire Builder Rats. Once you got the Empire Builder mark, you were property of the Empire.

As the ominous group approached, Donovan watched several of his fellow captives get their mark. It hurt like hell. Some teens sobbed, others cried out, one or two others passed out from the pain and wound. The hold quickly filled with the rank odor of cooked flesh. Captain Lepps got in the face of each teen as if sizing them up for their new "honor." Though his face was covered by a mask, he seemed clearly disappointed at every turn. Just a couple of boys away from Donovan, the teen caught ear of his offhanded comments: "Pathetic," and "You'll be back in the Sewer as soon as I can flush my loo," were among the captain's words of encouragement.

Donovan struggled to hide his pack and tried to sneak the book into his jumpsuit. The sight of the dozens of dim red lights of monitor cameras blinking overhead stopped him cold. Captain Lepps took note of Donovan's look of hesitation and slowly began to walk over. A tall, striking, long-haired teen next to Donovan grabbed the book from Donovan's hidden hands and pulled it behind his own back, where he passed it a couple of willing kids away. Donovan glared and was about to protest, but the long-haired teen gave him a reassuring wink.

"Get the rest of your junk into the flashers, quickly," the teen said directly. "Make a show of it."

Lepps casually walked over as Donovan dropped the pickax into the flasher hole. He then stopped the lad from putting the rest of the pack into the incineration device. Lepps picked the bag up and then flipped open his helmet shield. The captain's eyes and demeanor were even colder than his faceless helmet. He was tall and icy cool, with platinum blonde hair and wolf-blue eyes. He never blinked and eyed Donovan's every subtle reaction as he looked through the backpack. It was empty. Lepps paused to raise an eyebrow and Donovan just gave him a subtle shrug in reply. The act of defiance wasn't lost on the other guards, and one of them angrily raised his Iron. Instead of letting the guard have his fun, Lepps waved him off and then personally patted Donovan down. He again found nothing but was clearly suspicious. But before Lepps could say or do more, a frightened Sewer Rat just three boys away tried to break free of the laser manacle and was beaten down for his fear and defiance. He was then shocked to within inches of his life and, like Donovan's cohort, dumped through a trap door to the street below.

While Lepps was occupied, the teen that had helped Donovan retrieved the book from the others and passed it back to Donovan, who stashed it in his new jumpsuit pocket. Donovan didn't know what to say or why he was being helped. Puzzled, he glanced at his new friend, who just looked forward with a sly grin. "Benny," he whispered. "Thank you, Benny," he coached Donovan. Benny had ice water in his veins. Donovan liked him instantly.

By the time Captain Lepps had refocused on Donovan, the backpack was down the flasher too. With nothing else to do now, Lepps motioned for the manacle to skip a few kids and come straight to Donovan, where Lepps personally shoved Donovan's arms into the binders. As Lepps hoped for a reaction, Donovan took the mark without so much as a blink, his defiant eyes stayed locked on Lepps the entire time. This was Donovan's first real taste of the Empire, and it disgusted him. Lepps paused on Donovan as the manacle team moved over to Benny.

"You're either going to be trouble," Lepps rumbled through an insincere smirk, "or you're going to win your freedom." He paused again. "I'm not sure which will be worse for you." A hint of a cruel kind of smile crept across Lepps's face. "Or for us."

Donovan glanced towards Benny, who looked back with fire and mischief in his eyes. For some reason, it emboldened Donovan more. Lepps started to turn but remained, hoping for some final reaction from Donovan. He wanted the boy to challenge him. Donovan obliged. He just calmly looked back into Lepps's unblinking eyes. "Freedom or death, sir."

Lepps blinked, then almost smiled—but didn't. Then, he simply moved on. Donovan's inner pen was flying from that moment.

'Twas a minute away from becomin' a wanted man...now, I was f'ever a marked one, but t'thing about marked men is thus, we've nothing much left to lose.

Benny took his Empire Builder mark with a whimsical wink in Donovan's direction. Donovan hoped to meet Benny again soon.

Then, the large Imperial Catcher suddenly shuddered and rose quickly, forcing the human cargo to hang on to the walls or each other. The only place to get a look at what was happening was up and through the open roof of the transport. High above, a massive set of doors burst open in the distance, and a bright beam of sunlight seemed to probe the hold as if searching its contents. For Donovan and the others, looking toward it felt like coming up from the bottom of a cold lake, the light and warmth growing slowly from a tiny filtered dot as it neared.

When a Sewer Rat gets picked as an Empire Builder, they give you a number... 'n' a uniform... 'n' lift you up into t'light... like it's a Goddamn resurrection....

4

LIBERTATEM

As the Empire Builder Transport slowly passed through the threshold and entered the light, high panels on its walls flew down. The sudden glare was instantly blinding to the Rats, who had lived most of their young lives in near perpetual darkness. As Donovan's eyes slowly adjusted, he caught his first glimpse of what rode upon the back of the Under City as if it were an old mule. His mouth dropped open as the glass and steel spires of Empire City rose into the distance like a mountain range. The buildings were massively palatial in every direction, cathedral-like, and looked like the towers and parapets of a vast and monumental castle. They reflected the sky in a patchwork of blue and silver, they glowed like precious stones or ice sculptures.

The hulking transport then turned to the side, revealing a vast coastline far in the distance. This area was far different than the city beyond; it was industrial land. There, smoke billowed from dark and massive structures and reached into the sky like the dirty, unmistakable fingers of foundries and steelworks. It was the Colonies, just as Donovan's father had foretold, the worker's backbone of the Empire, separated by class and a massive wall.

The Colonies, Rush's words had taught his son, were merely a leg up from the Sewers, full of black marketeers, traders, and dealers. The Empire kept them in careful competition and trade, suppressing prices for goods and services meant for the Empire, with just enough lawlessness and corruption to make serving the Empire's needs worth the while of the few Colonials in power. Rush had written that the Colonies were a real ticket to the Empire, as anybody who could extort enough coin from the Colonials and then pay off the Empire could buy a ticket to a better life. Better to rule in Hell than to serve in Heaven.

"That's where I'm headed," Benny half-whispered to Donovan as he followed the boy's sightline.

"T'Colonies?" Donovan challenged the teen from the side of his mouth. There was no way Benny could ever get there now.

"Gonna run them someday." Benny nodded like it was already done.

It had taken Donovan nearly six years to convince his friends back in Dogue Run to think like that. Still, he had to go it alone. Here was Benny, a kindred spirit.

"Where you from, Benny?" Donovan smiled now.

"There." Benny nodded towards the Colonies.

Donovan's eyes opened wider with questions.

"'Til my old man knuck got us tossed into t'Sewers," Benny groused through the painful memory. "He spent all his days thievin' on t'Black Market 'n' every night drinkin' himself into his altitudes. After a few too many fortnights o' debauchery 'n' knuckery, and about to get t'whole Colonial Council in t'muck, Governor Cooke o' Rhodes turned him in to t'Lawbrokers to save his own neck."

Donovan stared at the distant sight and thought about the next passage for his father's journal.

My old man wrote that t'Colonies were nuthin' but a greedy and soulless middle class o' sorts... t'industrial backbone o' t'Empire... everythin' from gangs to businesses, factories, 'n' merchants. They were fed a slick marketed diet o' fear and hope... shite like "support t'Magistrate long enough an' ya might get t'live in Empire City someday..." t'was nothin' but bloody lies for them too... but t'was a step up from a gutter.

Benny knew about it maybe e'en more than my old man, but Benny and I were about t'go our separates. Rats were meant t'be kept apart... n' this trip t'was surely our first and only assembly.

On that thought, the massive Empire Builder Transport ship lurched and turned, and the sight of the Colonies was quickly gone. Donovan glanced down at the still-bleeding Empire Builder tattoo on his wrist and knew that he would likely never get the chance to see the Colonies now. He didn't have much time to dwell on it. In another moment, the giant airship tilted forward. They were landing.

"Got a name, Empire Builder?" Benny prodded him.

"Donovan Washington Rush, sir."

"There's a load o' words." Benny smirked. "I'm just gonna call ya Donnie."

Donovan liked that. It's what his father had called him too.

After settling with a thunderous bang, the side of the transport vessel dropped away like a military landing craft, and Imperial Troops flooded in.

"LET'S GO, EMPIRE BUILDERS! FORM A LINE!" the guards screamed out as they shoved their new workforce by hand or, if too slow, the end of an electrified Barking Iron. Donovan and Benny were quickly separated.

"Nice knowin' ya, Donnie," Benny said as he was ushered away.

Donovan was then placed in a line of boys a couple rows from Benny. He barely had enough time to look around, but there he was, in the Empire. The Transport had dropped them in a massive courtyard adorned with giant Empire logos and flags so large they slapped like waves crashing when they billowed in the wind. The courtyard was closed in on three sides and quite secure. On the fourth side, a massive gate led out to a phalanx of transport busses. Captain Lepps moved into the crowd with a tablet-shaped device, scanning each teen's tattoo and directing them to a particular transport. When the blueish beam hit the tattoo, it revealed a hidden barcode embedded in the crown. Donovan wasn't just marked, he was catalogued. Captain Lepps lingered in front of Donovan for an extra beat. The information on his tablet seemed to please him.

"Rush—Magistrate Tower. Transport Number Two," he said with a Cheshire grin as he spun Donovan by the shoulders and shoved him on. "You so much as sneeze in there and they'll fit you for a necktie," he chuckled.

Donovan was shoved along again by some more Imperial Guards and sent off towards the gate and his transport. His mind swam through ever more questions. *Magistrate Tower? That sounds like a government building for certain. Am I being put to work in the very center of the Imperial government? Is my very first Empire Builder assignment to work for the very enemy of all my father stood for?*

Boarding Empire Builder Transport Number Two, Donovan would have nothing to distract him from the questions. The transport had no windows and dim interior lights not unlike the darkness of the Sewers. Still, very much like the bits of the Empire Donovan had now seen, it was pristine and polished. Donovan knew it was all just mere appearance. The Transport was little more than a hopeless prison bus where Donovan and fourteen other teens sat in silence. As the transport machine rumbled to life and began to move, Donovan took in every sensation and sound. He had never been in a motorized land craft before. The ride was smooth and strangely comforting. It was dead quiet.

The whole trip took about forty minutes in all, and when the doors opened again, an even brighter light seemed to pierce the darkness. Seated halfway inside the Transport, Donovan had to follow a few other Empire Builders out and into that light. The image outside took a few moments to sink in, partly from adjusting to the brightness and partly just to process that it was indeed reality.

Towering above the Transport was an impossibly large and tall glass and gold building curved into the shape of a crown. Eight immense jeweled columns surrounded it and rose to eight massive spires. Between the spires hung a huge glassed-in archway. The arch stretched from one side of the structure to the other and atop it was an iron cross emblem. The Magistrate Tower was exactly as it sounded. This was the palace of His Magistrate, William Frederick the Third.

As Donovan was led inside, he saw that his Transport sat on one of eight bridges that connected the tower to the rest of Empire City. Each bridge led to one of the massive spires. As they moved down their particular bridge, Donovan and his fellow Empire Builders were shoved towards a security gate where they were to be searched again. Donovan's heart sank as he realized his father's book was about to be lost. He looked skyward and to either side for some possible escape. The bridge's railing was only a hundred feet away, and Donovan thought about leaping to his death. Then, he caught sight of a window high up on a neighboring building. There, a couple of tiny Empire City children made faces at him and the other Empire Builders. Not getting the reaction they hoped for, they flashed Donovan an obscene gesture before their mother appeared with a cold glare and pulled them out of sight. The image made Donovan focus on the security gate. *Even if they take my father's book,* he thought, *they cannot take away his ideas.*

As he neared the security gate, Donovan glanced up at the Magistrate Tower. High above, he could make out the shapes of several royal blue-clad Empire Builders a hundred floors up, traversing the exterior of the nearest spire, wire brushes and high-speed metal scrapers in hand. They were cleaning the pigeon droppings off a series of rooftop statues on the nearest spire. Just then, one of the workers lost his grip, slipped, and his safety harness broke. Only Donovan noticed as the body plummeted silently and hit the bridge to the side of them. As he entered the gate, Donovan managed a glance back and had just enough time to spot a young couple recoil from the sight before two faceless Imperial guards rushed over to pitch the body through a Sewer grate where Donovan knew it would find its way back home.

"Keep moving, EYES FORWARD!" a guard prodded Donovan with his Barking Iron.

Empire Building was no resurrection. T'was a death sentence. 'Tis wot it means t'get picked. 'Tis freedom in t'Empire: freedom AS death.

Inside the gate, Donovan was stopped and searched by the Magistrate Guards. They were far different from the Imperial Guard; their armor and uniforms were a strange blend of history and technology—leather, gold trim, bits of armor, and flak jacket all blended together. Their faces were also visible but under low feathered helmets. One of the Magistrate guards quickly found Donovan's book but only cursorily looked through it. Thinking it some harmless journal that had not aroused the interest of the Empire Transport Guards, he returned it with hardly a reaction of his own. Donovan was then handed a window-cleaning device and equipment bag and sent towards a bank of elevators.

Donovan's assigned room was high up in the glass archway, he guessed near the very apex. He and three other Empire Builders were led by a single large guard. Clearly, the Empire expected no trouble here, nobody would dare, and none would survive such treachery. Donovan was certain that every movement was guarded, watched, and any action would have provoked an immediate and deadly response. He took note of government officials, cameras, and places where hidden weapons and security devices might be stashed. He didn't have the time or opportunity to look out from the arch, but from what glances he could steal during his walk, he marveled how Empire City spread out as far as the eye could see in every direction. It was like a vast jewelry box had been opened under the sun. The city shapes spread brilliant colors and light in every direction. It almost hurt to look at.

Donovan watched as each of the other teens was pushed towards a room along the way, which left Donovan alone with the guard. They passed lavish works of art, paintings depicting the glory and power of the Empire and several more uniformed men and women all dressed in colorful long coats. Donovan noted how his own former Sewer garb looked like a mirrored and tortured ghost of Imperial dress. The archway hall's inhabitants didn't so much as raise an eyebrow Donovan's way. It was as if he didn't exist to them. Maybe he, like his father, was now just a ghost as well.

Ahead, a large archway beckoned. Beneath it was a huge dark wooden door with graceful benches on either side. The guard approached and the door opened automatically. He pulled Donovan through and into an immense room filled with flat-panel screens, opulent furnishings, and other adornments of glistening, precious metals, gold, and polished stone. The Imperial Palace guard abruptly stopped just inside the door as if he himself was allowed no further. He then shoved Donovan towards an entire wall of windows.

"One single smudge and I'll toss your knuck ass out the window myself," the guard chuckled coldly. "A shortcut back to the hole."

Having never seen nor used the strange window-cleaning device before, Donovan instantly smudged the first window he touched. He glanced back at the guard, who grinned and took out his even more deadly-looking Barking Iron. After a few moments of struggling with the cleaning device, Donovan got the hang of it and was off. After perfectly cleaning the first window, Donovan again spied the guard who scowled, upset that his chance for cruel discipline was gone. The lad returned to his task. *This isn't so terrible,* he thought. He was growing curious as to what might happen next.

As he moved to the next window, a portly man in a lush green velvet waistcoat, ruffled white shirt, and light blue pants entered the massive room. He was carrying a stack of parchment papers and an electronic tablet computer. Donovan could only spy the man's faint reflection in the bright windows as he moved behind him. He was older and of dark complexion. For a moment, the man's appearance reminded Donovan of the Sewers, where humanity was such a mélange of skin tones, shapes, and sizes, unlike the paler monotone he'd already seen in Empire City. Where Donovan came from, only access to coin and connections separated people. Aside from those, they were most certainly all in the same situation.

The man paused by the Imperial Palace guard and stopped to watch Donovan for a beat. Suddenly unnerved and curious, Donovan slowed his work to pause on the man's reflection. It prompted the already irritated guard to immediately take a step towards the teen.

"What's the problem!" the guard growled as he extended his Iron and came up behind Donovan. "Does the Rat need a little motivation?"

The man in the green coat watched as the guard raised his barking Iron. He then cleared his throat and the guard stopped. Donovan picked up his pace accordingly and the guard lowered the weapon. This new man's air of authority gave Donovan some comfort that at least in this high hall of Imperial Government, cruelty wasn't always the norm it seemed to be everyplace else Donovan had lived and seen.

Donovan completed the second large pane of glass and moved on to the next. The guard moved to keep pace. The Imperial official took a few moments to settle into a side desk and write some notes on his tablet using a form of electronic quill. The device fascinated Donovan. It was similar to what he used in the Sewers, yet vastly technological and mysterious. The guard spent more time watching the official than Donovan and, in the next moment, Donovan stole another glance around the rest of the room.

At one far end was a giant ornate desk of carved wood and gold leaf. Beyond it at a far wall sat a massive high-backed throne of silver, blue, and gold. Donovan wondered if it were possible that he was inside the Magistrate's chamber, the throne room of William Frederick the Third, ruler of the Empire. The government official raised a wary eyebrow as he noticed Donovan pausing to look at the throne, but the look wasn't meant for Donovan; it was meant for the guard. As the guard noticed Donovan stop, he fired up his Barking Iron again and raised it to strike.

"Guard?" the official inquired calmly.

The Palace guard froze and turned.

"Must you lurk about so?" The elder man rose from the desk and strolled over.

The guard suddenly blinked, worried that he'd done something wrong.

The official walked straight past Donovan and up to the guard. "Let me put this another way." The official looked down his nose. "Get out. I can guard him myself."

The guard backed up a step and smudged Donovan's first window with his backside. He looked back at the mark with wide eyes as Donovan cleaned it for him. The official seemed suddenly amused by it all.

"Yes sir, Dr. Franklin...." the guard quickly bowed and rushed out.

Franklin calmly turned and went back to his desk and papers. Donovan watched for a beat as the man brushed aside his coattails, sighed, and sat. Franklin then glanced at the boy and casually waved his hand in a "carry on" gesture. He even smiled slightly as he pulled a pair of eyeglasses from his jacket and set them at the base of his nose.

Donovan worked even more diligently now as if to pay back Franklin's kindness but he was sure to keep a wary eye on the man. Franklin, for his part, was busy writing away on his tablet.

Franklin then stopped suddenly, pulled off his glasses, and rubbed his eyes and chin. He then looked up at Donovan; something in his own secretive scribblings had connected to the image of the lad. Franklin put down his digital quill and stood up.

"You, Empire Builder...come here...." His voice was gentle, almost playful.

Donovan stopped cold and looked. To Franklin's amusement, he scanned the room as if Franklin was calling for another. The government man simply smiled and curled his index finger in a beckoning motion. "Come on."

Fearing some kind of trick, Donovan checked the door before slowly approaching. Franklin walked over and met him halfway across the marble floor.

"What is your name, sir?" Franklin met Donovan eye to eye. Franklin smiled as Donovan paused on the word "sir." He raised an eyebrow as if to say, "I'm waiting."

"Donovan Washington Rush, sir," the teen replied softly.

Franklin blinked. "Rush?" His expression turned inward. "Rush, you say?"

Donovan watched the man's wheels turning. Where was this going? Franklin then turned to the side and paced a few steps away towards the huge wall of windows. He looked out across the endless sprawl of city. "Rush." He clasped his hands together over his chest and tapped the fingers of one atop the other.

With Franklin's back turned, Donovan glanced again at the Magistrate's throne. Franklin turned back and followed the boy's eyes until the now-frightened Donovan looked back. He was caught.

"It's just a chair, Mr. Rush." Franklin said it offhand.

Donovan tensed for some form of rebuke or discipline. When none came, he hastily went back to work. "Yes, sir."

"Guard's no longer here." Franklin waited until Donovan stopped on his innermost thoughts. "Sit if you want..." he offered plainly.

Donovan pretended not to hear and kept working.

"Go on!" Franklin finally thundered.

Unnerved, Donovan turned. Franklin waited impatiently. "Are you ordering me, sir?" was all the boy could mutter.

Franklin looked away to his papers. He seemed disappointed. "Fine, then don't." He picked up his quill stylus and went back to writing. He spoke to the papers. "If you'd like to try it, you are free to do so."

Donovan glanced back at the ornate throne. Franklin eyed him with a soft smirk. "I guarantee it'll fit your ass just well as the Magistrate's."

Donovan fought back a smile as Franklin looked up at him. The two locked eyes and Franklin arched his brows towards the throne. Donovan took a step for it and Franklin nodded, his eyes twinkling. Donovan humored him by gently dropping his butt to one of the throne's large arms. Franklin frowned.

"But I'm just a Sewer Rat, Dr. Franklin, sir."

Franklin put down his pen, stood up, and walked over. He grabbed the teen by the shoulders and leaned him back into the Magistrate's throne.

"Being poor is no shame, my boy." Franklin smiled over him before his look grew serious. "But being ashamed of being poor... *that* is shameful."

Franklin then paced away to the huge windows overlooking Empire City. Donovan instantly flew up to his feet.

"Sometimes, I worry about the Empire, lad...the Colonies... and the Sewer Rats..." he mused.

"Sir?" Donovan cautiously approached.

Franklin kept his eyes on the Empire. "When you use your money and your power to buy your freedom and your safety on the backs of others," he turned, "you don't really deserve either, do you?"

Franklin paced back over to Donovan and reached into his waistcoat. There, he retrieved a small golden Empire pin, the same stylized crown set in precious metal and jewels.

"I may be in this Empire, but I was born into work and service." Franklin smiled softly, completely unashamed of the pedestrian sound of it. "Did you know that I created a newspaper of the seemingly ordinary and mundane, the stories of those who work here, the minsters and clerks and minor officials, whose lives and outlook on life, it turns out, completely fascinate those of power and privilege?" Franklin's eyes sparkled with mischief as he took Donovan by the arm and led him across the room. "It's as if the aristocracy realizes how much they envy those of lesser rank, almost wish for such a simpler outlook and those who have so much less pomp and circumstance to worry about on a daily basis."

Donovan searched Franklin's eyes. *Why is he telling me this?*

"I've written books on it, given lectures about what makes us the same and how what divides us is mere convention, mere appearance, created by some to have official cause and permission to rule over others." Franklin's eyes opened widely as if the words still amazed him as much as they now did Donovan. "And every-body loves every word, never stopping to think of how wrong it all is, how inequitable, how destined for failure." Franklin chuckled. "They don't even see it as the warning I intend. If that's not an Empire destined to fail, I do not know what is."

Franklin could see the fear building in Donovan's eyes. He could see the distrust and expectation of impending doom highlighted by Donovan's wary and constricted sips of breath. A sad and caring look came to Franklin's face as he slid his grasp down to Donovan's wrist. There, he pressed the golden pin into the boy's palm and smiled. It seemed wrong to Donovan, replacing the star of his father's book with a symbol of the Empire, but something about Franklin and his words seemed to make it ok. *How could it be just a trick?* Here in the Empire was a man who thought and spoke like Donovan's own father. Maybe there was more hope for the Sewers than Donovan could ever imagine.

"It's just a simple gift." Franklin winked. "Keep it always to remind you of my words." Franklin looked into the teen's eyes. "Is that alright?"

Donovan's face was a confused mess. He could barely even nod.

"Know anything of freedom, Donovan Washington Rush?" Franklin's expression turned more serious.

"A little."

"Do you now? What do you know of freedom, Mr. Rush?" Franklin nodded his head to give silent permission to speak.

"Freedom's not given, sir…'tis taken…." Donovan barely got out the words.

Franklin's eyes lit up. "That's right, lad, it is!" He closed Donovan's hand on the pin and patted the lad on the chest. "We were meant to fight for such things…."

With that, Franklin simply brushed his hand over Donovan's shoulder and gave the lad a reassuring pat. He then calmly walked to his desk, gathered his belongings, and left the throne room. Dumbfounded and with nothing else to do, Donovan went back to work on the windows.

Out in the hall, Franklin walked over to the Imperial guard, who was waiting for Donovan to finish his tasks.

"What shall we do with him, my lord?" The guard stood firm, hoping for some command to punish the boy.

"When he's done, send him back."

"Back?" The guard blinked.

"Back home." Franklin brushed past the guard.

"But Lord Franklin? That's not…"

Franklin stopped and turned. His look was as unpleasant as his voice. "You asked me my wish and I have given it to you, or are you more interested in asking questions than following orders? I've already made the proper official notification."

"Of course," the guard stuttered. "It's just that…"

"What?" Franklin glared at him now, creating an awkward standoff.

"It's most irregular."

"It is within my authority, is it not?" Franklin narrowed his eyes.

"Of course." The once-imposing guard blinked, bowed, and moved back into the throne room. Franklin stretched his neck and back as if they weighed heavily on his rounded frame. He then took a seat on one of the waiting benches in the hall. He went back to his journal.

I instantly noticed the lad at the window when I entered the Lord's chamber. He was different than

the other Empire Builders I've met over the years.
He met my gaze straight away, didn't look away,
barely a flinch nor a blink. There was a spirit to the
lad, an air of something brave and honorable.

Most Rats just want to swim and eat their way out
of their lot. This one is quite a different sort. Rush, he
said his name was. I can only hope it to be true that,
somehow in the shadows of this Empire, light may
still shine, and this lad may carry it.

If it's true there's a relation, then this has been a
very long day coming. I once knew a Dr. Rush, a man
of the Empire in good standing until, in the Magistrate's eyes, he became a rabble-rouser, a staunch
champion of the less fortunate, the Colonials and the
Rats. Revolution, he warned, was in the offing.
"Beware the three tyrannies," was the doctor's familiar refrain. "Beware the tyranny of royalty, of
aristocracy, and, most diabolical and insidious, the
subtle tyranny of economy. Beware any system of
government that seeks to concentrate the power of the
state in an ever-shrinking pyramid of control and
influence. The further up the apex goes, the steeper
the sides become and the more who fall off attempt-
ing to reach the summit. The more bodies to
accumulate at the base, the happier the people are
accepting crumbs and trinkets to ease their want and
disenfranchisement." I agreed with him but dared
not do so publicly. I have been called a reckless man
on occasion, but I'm no suicidal fool. Suppose I
prefer my crumbs and trinkets over death.

Several years ago, Dr. Rush was presented with a trip to the Sewers for his thoughts. I helped secure it; otherwise, he'd have been hung. Strange fortunes indeed to have brought another of the same name to my awareness. I had to give the lad that Magistrate pin, so I could keep track of him, see what seeds my late friend may have sown. What happened to Dr. Rush and his cause changed my view of the Empire forever. I now see it for what it is: an enslaved state. Enslaved by three tyrannies. This lad may be my best chance either way, to help reform or to root out another revolution if need be. I just need to determine which is the lesser of two evils.

On his tablet device, Dr. Franklin opened a special secure window into the Magistrate's mainframe. He then opened a private tracking box and pulled up a map of the local area of Empire City. It showed a crown representation of the Magistrate pin hovering in the looming shape of the Magistrate Tower. Franklin labeled the dot as "DWR" for Donovan Washington Rush.

5

A FIRST CROSSING

Rhodes Colony was on the marshy northeastern coast of the Colonies and was one of the main international shipping ports for the Empire. The entire economy of Rhodes was based on trade with other colonies and foreign concerns. Along with Conn's Colony to the south and Bay's just to the north, Rhodes was a bustling black market of shipping and fishing. What you could leverage (or even plunder) from your rivals to keep prices down meant big sales to the Empire and industrial colonies. Those sales and deals, in turn, meant favorable treatment and opportunity from Empire agents happy to look the other way on illegal maneuvers as long as the bottom line favored them.

In downtown Prudence Town, a moderately luxurious high-rise mostly reserved for affluent colonials hid a few more perks of the system. The upscale address also contained a few smaller and more mundane apartments set aside for Lawbrokers, Watch-man Lee Cruz among them. The very afternoon Donovan Rush cleaned the Magistrate's windows, Watchman Lee Cruz stood on her balcony and sipped from a mug of char, a colonial drink consisting of dark tea spiked with sugar and grain alcohol.

As she watched the burnt orange sunset to the west, Cruz pondered how she never quite felt comfortable in her special housing, though she did love the view. Her balcony faced the bulk of Rhodes and the far larger Bay's Colony to the distant north. The vast and mirage-like mountain range that was Empire City was set behind her building, across the massive retaining walls of the North Colonies and then across a vast no-man's-land of power, sewage, and waste-reclamation plants. Ten stories down on the Prudence Town streets below, the flashing blue lights of a Constabulary cruiser flashed. From her high vantage point, Cruz watched as two more Constable cars moved from different points of the tangled city grid, converging on a single point—somebody was running from the law. Her mind raced along with the pursuit.

On another grid, the grid of her memory, the same blue lights flashed as Cruz raced her own dark unmarked Constabulary car down the narrow cobblestone streets of the past. Inside the car and on a screen in front of her, the name "KZ" flashed with the last known photo of a powerful Rhodes black marketeer. Barely nineteen years old at the time, KZ Fayette was already near the top of the Colonial black market hierarchy and as striking to look at as she was dangerous to deal with. Half Huaxian and half Capes, both of which were historical adversaries of the Empire, KZ's connections to goods and governments ran deep, all the way to her home country Huaxia, a far-off empire to the east. Huaxia was a manufacturing powerhouse and Capes was a cunning political power. Combined, they made for perfect partners in Black-Flag smuggling, designed not just on the notion of profit but also on shared economic power and regional control.

On this particular night, Cruz recalled how KZ had run afoul of the local Port Council of Merchants, which was little more than a Colony- and Empire-sanctioned mess, thrown together to control corruption just enough to keep both the Black Markets and the Empire properly fed. KZ had used her connections to expose three high-up council members for taking bribes in order to divert a massive shipment of offshore metals, which could be used for precious electronics, straight into her warehouses. It wasn't particularly illegal if the end result was Empire profit, but it was against the local rules just the same. As far as the Lawbrokers and the Constabulary were concerned, anybody was guilty until the best deal was cut, at which point they'd back off.

Cruz was at the waterfront when the three members of the council were detained, but she quickly realized that KZ and her crew could use the distraction to move on the shipments just offshore. Without the blessing of her superiors, Cruz went for the glory. She was three years younger then, far less worldly, and emboldened to take her shot. It very well could have been her ticket to the Empire. She had allies at the Constabulary too, among them a long-time Lawbroker named Richard Montgomery who, though he'd been passed up for promotion, was a friend of Lord Constable Thomas Hall Gage, the head of Rhodes Colony's highest law-enforcement organization. Only problem now was whether or not "Monty" could get her out of trouble, if this was the career mistake she knew it might be.

Cruz recalled how she tensely gripped the wheel of her cruiser as she darted through the cramped cobblestone streets and past other cars, trucks, and animal-drawn carts. She was committed, her entire future now riding with her. Just at the edge of her vision, a dashboard monitor showed the target motorcycle in front of her moving and turning in a navigation system kind of map. Her radio crackled to life with an angry voice.

"*Watchman Cruz.*" *The sandpaper voice of Constable Gage dug into her ears.* "*Who authorized this pursuit?*"

Before she could make up some excuse, Cruz noted as her monitor map now contained two more blue dots to her one, closing in from the sides. They were marked LB UNIT 1 and LB UNIT 2. Apparently, two other Lawbrokers had similar delusions of grandeur and, from the sound of Gage's voice, Cruz was not meant to be one of them. So much for connections. Suddenly, convinced that maybe the Constable himself was part of the mess, Cruz felt it had all become extremely personal.

"*Suspect vehicle locked!*" *she barked back at Gage. She wasn't going to stop.*

"*I am ordering you to stand down,*" *Gage shouted.*

As Cruz's attention lingered on the other two Constable cars closing, she almost didn't see a small group of pedestrians enter the road just beyond a blind turn. She swerved at the last second, blasting through a row of sidewalk carts and boxes of stacked goods.

"*DAMMIT!*" *she yelled as debris flew past her view, partly out of fear and partly because she'd just lost ground on KZ.*

As the two blue dots of her competitors closed from the sides, KZ took a wrong turn down a twisted side street. Cruz knew the area well and quickly formulated a shortcut to the halfway point of the escape route. With luck, she'd be right behind her suspect in a few tense seconds.

"*Gotcha.*" *She smiled as she flew into the shortcut. A few seconds later, she pulled into the side street and right behind KZ on her sleek and silent electric motorbike.*

That's when one of the other Constabulary cruisers came in from the side and T-boned Cruz's car. The impact and airbags knocked the breath out of the watchman as both her and the vehicle pinwheeled. In dragged-out seconds, Cruz regained her bearings and grabbed the wheel and desperately tried to control the spin as she missed more people and vehicles. Then, from a small driveway ahead of her, a passenger vehicle pulled out. The crash was violent and loud before the world went eerily silent and black.

Watchman Lee Cruz awoke under a blanket of broken glass, a smoking forward airbag, and her own blood. The first thing she could focus her eyes on was the sheer mayhem of the crash. There were shattered sidewalk displays and vendor markets. Fish, fruit, and assorted goods had been fired all over the block as if from a powerful explosion. Tilting her aching and bleeding head to the side, Cruz realized that she had been hit by another Constabulary car, but with their built-in collision warnings and tracking systems, how could that be?

She then spotted the younger Silas Tarleton running over. Tarleton and Cruz had graduated in the same Watchman class, but it always seemed Tarleton had some hidden advantage. Cruz never knew how deep his connections ran, but it didn't stop her from the competition. It was going to taste sweeter when she finally bested him. Even in her daze, Cruz was angry to see him here; it seemed to Cruz as if Tarleton had been hanging over her every move since training school. Her anger lasted until she noticed the car she'd run into.

Behind the wheel and slumped to the side, Cruz stared into the wide, lifeless eyes of a young woman. As more Constabulary cars arrived, Cruz grunted and pushed her way out of her broken vehicle. Tarleton reached for her but she yanked away, her mind elsewhere. Bloody and woozy, she staggered to the nameless woman's car.

"How the hell did you run into me?" Cruz glanced over at Tarleton icily as she stumbled on. "Didn't you see me on the scope?!?"

Tarleton followed her a few steps. "GODDAMMIT, Lee! The tracking system malfunctioned! I didn't know you were there!"

Cruz left Tarleton standing in the street and crept over to the other car and the dead woman. Each step closer to the sight, her strength abandoned her and she stumbled and fell onto the side fender. She looked into the crushed passenger compartment and saw that the woman was pregnant. Her palms instantly few up to her face, her knees buckled, and she slid onto the street.

"I killed her...I killed them both..." she began to mutter.

As Tarleton came over along with some other Watchmen, Cruz sank into shuddering despair. She pulled at her hair and face and wailed. "OH MY GOD! I KILLED THEM!"

"We'll take care of it..." Tarleton offered as the moment hit him too. "Lee. We can take care of this."

Nothing but cries.

"Cruz! Do you hear me?!?"

She was inconsolable.

"Constable Gage can fix this!"

Cruz's thoughts went straight to Monty.

Cruz watched from her balcony as the triangulating blue lights below converged but did not crash. KZ had gone on that day to cut a deal with some powerful Colonial merchants who were all too happy to get three of their competitors to take a fall. KZ was far more powerful and even, to some extent, accepted by the Empire. Cruz wasn't so lucky.

Tarleton advanced quickly through the ranks afterwards, while the chase incident and aftermath weighed heavily on Cruz and was used to hold her back. The favor done by the Constabulary in making the whole thing go away also left her beholden to Gage and the Constabulary. Cruz often wondered why both helping her and controlling her was seemingly so important. Was there something about her that they feared? Or was somebody even higher up watching after her? She fancied the second scenario, but knew the first was far more likely. The whole inequitable and random mess of it all led her thoughts back to Donovan Washington Rush, the terrified Sewer Rat who had escaped her and Lawbroker Tarleton just by sheer chance.

She walked back inside her apartment and sprawled her long body over the couch. Something about her next sip of char tasted bad and she set the mug down on her zinc coffee table. She needed to figure something out, an item that had been bothering her since Tarleton's and her Lawbroker patrol in the Sewers.

Cruz rose and walked across her small apartment and slipped behind her desk and her Constabulary portal computer. After logging in, she ran the feed from the day's patrol. She stopped the recording on the frightened face of Donovan Washington Rush. There was no name to the face, no identification. As luck had it, Lawbroker Lieutenant Tarleton's need for more and bigger fish had spared Donovan a closer inspection. Spared him from Tarleton, but not from Watchman Lee Cruz.

She decided to run his face through the recognition database, partly hoping to find nothing. But something about him had already been found, she just didn't know what. Cruz was in for a surprise when a match came up. It was a sad surprise. Donovan Washington Rush had been identified by Perimeter Five security earlier in the day, breaking almost every rule of the Sewers and the Empire, yet there was no arrest or termination record. Cruz assumed he either got away or turned back—no harm, no foul. But then, another match popped up in her Constabulary display. Donovan was picked up as an Empire Builder just an hour later. Cruz thought about the irony—knuck one moment, condemned for something else entirely the next. Distressed, she shut down the computer and went back to the couch. Her char tasted just as bad, but she needed it just the same. She reached onto the coffee table and pulled up her personal tablet and began to write. There was nobody to talk to except herself.

In a society that celebrates neither freedom nor liberty, the liberty of complaining can be a dangerous and deadly affair. Yet any person, like a rat on a sinking ship, would never be denied the liberty of roaring as loud as they could to be saved from certain death, neither punished except by providence for taking desperate actions. I'm stuck, just as hard and fast as this boy is, trapped between the Colonies and the Empire.

We work for everything here, yet we get basically nothing save of things to chase; we make deals on everything. It's all a game of careful Imperial strategy, with Colonials and Sewer Rats alike watching each other. What clubs you join, who you associate with, who your friends are. Everything is branded here yet not owned—except by the Empire. We therefore pay into a vast system that bleeds us dry, so we have no choice but to skirt the law; there is no true opportunity here outside of rakes and profiteers.

The Colonial Council is a shadowy affair whose only true function is to create an air of propriety amongst thieves and knucks. Each colony is left by the Empire in a constant state of brutal and desperate competition. The Colonial leaders that steal the best and make the best deals in order to pass on vast savings and advantage to the Empire are rewarded with coin, power, and a leg up to the Empire itself. Such Colonial governors get more protection from Lawbrokers, more favorable outcomes if disputes reach the Magistrate's courts, and are allowed to skirt the laws even further in the name of Imperial profits.

The Empire has thusly set up the Colonial system as little more than lotteries and contests of deal-making, backstabbing, and bartering. It is a larger and more equitable system than the one they promise the Rats as Empire Builders. You work, you pay your taxes on everything, and somewhere at the end of the maze, you might get a big payoff of some reward and power. The taxes are the worst of it. Even if you don't think there's tax, there is—hidden in fractions of pence and such on food, water, and every service and system. And each and every mark in the ledger—those fractions of tax—goes on up the ladder to the Empire, where they feed the very few on the backs of the rest.

The money here doesn't truly go to the Colonies either, just a shred of the profit. It all goes to the Empire to pay for their peace and cleanliness and buildings and food and delicacies, fabulous clothes, private clubs, vacations, and security. Sure, some of us make it out of here more readily than Rats, but only fractionally so. What the vast hordes of us really get is a lifetime of debt—buying things to copy the Imperials, to look like them, drive craft like them. We actually give them more and more of our money to pretend to be them.

Fact is, an Empire needs slaves, those disenfran-chised just enough to direct their anger—to set up public displays of force and punishment. The rest mix that anger with hope, and those few individuals in power then use them for work. Those who work get just enough of a taste of power to go into indentured servitude to get the illusion of a chance to be free, which they will never get. And those still, like the Lawbrokers, those just below the power itself, are allowed to wield it, but never allowed to actually have it. We are all rats in a sense, all in the same maze, and the door has long since been written off the map. The most hopeless group of all are those like the young teen I saw today—this boy Rush—who seek the door long since closed, those who still have hope. They will pay the most.

As Lawbrokers, Watchmen, and Constables, we control the Barking Iron and have the power to condemn and capture in order to keep the peace, but this, too, is merely borrowed power. Like everything else, it is leased from the state.

When I saw Donovan Washington Rush in the Sewers today, he seemed as much an innocent victim of random events as the unborn child I killed those years ago. Now, his reward for his cry for liberty is a new life of slavery in the very Empire the strength of his back supports.

Looming over the northeast corner of the dark and dangerous Fairfax Square, the Dogue Run group home was an ancient and jagged structure. The five-story brick-and-wood brownstone was in a serious state of disrepair and leaned about ten degrees to the right, propped up by large reclaimed timbers taken from other fallen Rat nests. Ironically, the home was originally intended for orphaned and runaway teens. Years before in some vaguely democratic experiment, a ragtag Fairfax Council had intended the teens of the area to work in one of their many failed Empire-sanctioned Sewer work programs. That in and of itself wasn't a bad idea, even if it was just a way for the Empire to trick the Sewers into false hope, but there were two very real and destructive issues. First, the Council would only hand the workers a small fraction of what they got from the Empire, a few more to the Sewer Guards who kept order and control, and the rest to fund the greater Fairfax Militia, an army designed to protect one Sewer Land from the other. It was merely a shadow of the Empire's carefully crafted Colonial structure—control by division.

There were six lands in the Sewers, of varying degrees of loyalty to the Empire and loyalty to themselves. They were merely an incident or two from war at all times. Regardless of the motives behind the profits, the whole program turned into little more than a form of indentured servitude for Donovan and his friends. It was like a vast network of organized crime, almost a slave trade. It was designed that way. There was no real reward for fixing up the Sewer except the notion of keeping a vast prison cell orderly. Deal upon deal had to be cut with local Sewer Rats, too, for protection, and that too usually turned to extortion and bribery. As a result, the Fairfax Militia grew stronger as an Imperial Mule force. This, in turn, made the Fairfax area appear a more friendly and loyal Sewer Land to the Empire. It gave the Brothers and Sisters of the Sword some needed leeway, though it also placed the Dogue Run area under an increased measure of watch. *More eyes of the Empire.*

After reading from his father's book, Donovan was emboldened enough to seek out Rats of like mind to take over the group home by attrition. His Brothers and Sisters of the Sword worked with a part-time Sewer Guard turncoat named Knox, a younger teen Donovan had befriended a couple years earlier, and together with other teens more wary of Imperial influence, they moved on the home on their own, driving out the council to other opportunities.

It wasn't just the words of Dr. Rush that swayed the teens, either. Knox made a living as a shopkeeper and an archeologist of sorts. His family ran a small book and artifact shop that sold recycled old novels and trinkets to the slightly more affluent Sewer Rats, the ones that, like Donovan's brother Lar, farmed night-shades or dug in the Empire mines. Like Donovan, Knox too was hiding far more than he let on. Three years Donovan's junior, the rail-thin, fair-haired Knox seemed an old soul. Though he only admitted it to Donovan, it seemed that the resourceful Knox had been into several of the forbidden Perimeters of the Sewers and had traveled into the other five of the so-called Six Lands of the Underground.

In his scavenging travels, Knox had managed to find the ruins of old libraries and document storage houses, and, inside of those, found fragments of an even older culture and what seemed to be an earlier Empire. It was all only bits and scraps of history, tattered pages and fragments of larger volumes. Nothing had covers, everything was burnt, soiled, faint, and water-damaged, but one thing seemed clear: Knox, like Donovan's own father, claimed that the Sewers were the original Empire and that, by some cataclysm or class war, the present Empire rose.

Clearly, none of these books and texts were meant to survive, but Knox had carefully transcribed what he could and kept it safe. There were fragments of military guides on tactics and weapons the likes of which could be assembled from Sewer debris. Knox also found bits of writing on government and politics. Much of the material bore a striking resemblance to the writings of Donovan's father as it dealt with concepts like liberty and equality. *Had the elder Rush seen the same texts?* They looked nearly half a millennium old. Knox thought them at least as old. He also found remnants of his family history—or at least that's what he claimed the documents contained.

Knox fancied himself from Bay's Colony, though how exactly he got to the Sewers remained a mystery; he had, however, found a cache of documents that seemed to support his claims. When he met Donovan on one of the teen's early explorations, they hit it off and Knox became Donovan's confidant and spy. Through Knox, Donovan learned he could take over the group home and just how far he could push the law. When the opportunity arose, Donovan and his Brothers and Sisters of the Sword exposed the corrupted members of the Fairfax Council and then seized the building as their own. Enraged teens and Fairfax citizens conducted a public lynching of the offending group and the Fairfax Militia and Lawbroker overseers let it happen. It was good for security. Donovan's group was allowed control of the home and then, using documents from Knox as a guide, fashioned defenses and weapons. These "boom sticks" (as the teens called them) consisted of one-shot flintlocks that propelled a lead ball down a rifled tube. Knox kept the secret safe with the Sewer Guard and their Fairfax Militia. Nobody in the Guard or in the Lawbroker patrols realized that on any night or day, a half dozen or more armed sentries peered out from the fenced-in fifth-floor balcony. Their faces blacked out by charcoal, their boom sticks always at the ready. It was a fortress of subversion. So long as no Imperial laws were broken and all seemed well with Sewer Guard spies, it was nothing worth looking into, though on this night, there was a lot to be found.

The citizens of Dogue Run and Fairfax Flats never thought about it much; it was just a home for messed-up kids, and the kids were now in control. But more was going on inside the walls. Knox and Donovan had begun to spread the word through the Six Lands of the Sewers, into little groups like their own, carefully maneuvered into secret pods and cells, where there were no names and layers of complicated contact using only codes and numbers. Neither Donovan nor Knox knew how big or small the reach of their collected words, but it was all done according to Dr. Rush's plan. But plan for what, exactly? While the tiny taste of self-determination seized along with the Dogue Run home galvanized the group, it wasn't enough to have them thinking grander thoughts beyond the Sewers. Their comfort had been part of the motivation for Donovan to run.

On this particular night, inside the candlelit epicenter of the Dogue Run home, Donovan Washington Rush, now back in slightly newer and less-soiled Sewer clothing, paced by a battered brick wall covered with graffiti. Painted and scratched into the brick, along with the slogans and cryptic marks of the Brothers and Sisters of the Sword, was the familiar hand clutching the star icon along with the slogan "FREEDOM OR DEATH." A dozen teens sat around a large table on top of which was painted a rough version of the main map in Dr. Rush's book.

The room was a place of past glory and future hope, but tonight, it was the home of dread. Tonight, the members of the Brothers and Sisters of the Sword all looked up to their *de facto* leader with a mix of confusion and alarm. He'd risked not only his life by running, but theirs as well. His trip to the Empire was as troubling a turn as anything they knew.

Carr, a tough tomboy teen with long, matted dark hair pulled high on her head in a single ponytail, was the first to speak up. Her eyes never left the Empire Builder tattoo on Donovan's forearm as she spoke.

"Why'd they let you out, I wonder?" She glanced up into Donovan's eyes and then back to the inked mark on his arm. "No Empire Builder's ever come back." She was clearly suspecting a setup.

Donovan had no easy answer. "I told you, some Boss Dog Blue Coat commanded one o'his skunks t'send me back. Next I know, they locked me in a Catcher 'n' dumped me back...just past Auld Way."

"That's it?" She found it all too convenient.

"On my oath." Donovan didn't blink as his eyes wandered the other faces.

"Who?" Carr asked, even though the name was immaterial. "Who let you go?" She folded her arms expecting silence.

"His name was Franklin." Donovan shrugged, not sure why it was important.

For a few moments, the room fell silent on the name of an Imperial government official. Nobody had ever heard an Empire leader's name outside of Magistrate William Frederick the Third before.

Carr's brows furrowed more until they stuck in disbelief. She didn't like being challenged, less so with something so dangerous as being discovered as subversives against the Empire hanging over her head.

"'Tis obviously some kinda ruse!" Carr finally said it, using the room's collective thoughts against Donovan. "My wager's that Boss Dog's tryin' to draw us out...find t'nest." She eyed Donovan.

"They've known we're here for six years," Donovan groaned.

"This old Mule's using you," she ignored him. "Lawbrokers prolly movin' on us as we debate."

The room seemed to agree and banged out the sentiment on the tabletop using their open palms.

"I think not." Donovan met everyone's eyes as he paced behind Carr. "This Franklin, h'spoke of t'same things as t'book. H'spoke of freedom."

"A Blue Coat's freedom," Crispus snickered. The room nervously tapped out more of their agreement with the statement.

Donovan felt unsteady in the shifting sentiments. Johnay, a smaller, rounder teen with wispy reddish hair and ruddy skin, spoke up on his leader's behalf. Johnay was one of Donovan's staunchest supporters and had been with him from early on. It wasn't so much that Johnay supported Donovan outright, nor was Johnay the type to fight, but he'd read the elder Rush's book, too, and agreed with the sentiments. The idea of correcting the Empire's inequities motivated the lad. He was an intellectual, not a soldier. Still, Johnay's passion and thoughts carried a lot of sway with the group.

"Wot does Boss Dog know of it?" Johnay challenged Carr. "How? 'N' why now, all a sudden? They already had our leader in their grasp, as Donnie spake; they know where we are. They've known all along!" Johnay paced over to the darkened windows at the front end of the room and threw one open. "Officer of the watch?" he called into the darkness.

"Yes sir?" a sturdy teen voice responded.

"Anything out of t'ordinary?"

"All quiet, sir," the voice responded.

Johnay turned to Carr with a bow and a smirk.

"Maybe wot troubles us 'tis already inside," Carr said, glaring at Donovan.

As Johnay and Carr squared off, Donovan nervously placed his hands into the pockets of his long coat. There, he found the

Empire pin that Dr. Franklin had given him. He rolled it around his fingers and suddenly wondered if everything Carr said might be true. Had he just led the Empire straight to his home base?

Carr watched Donovan's inward moment of worry and caught his gaze. Carr thought she saw hesitation in Donovan's eyes and quickly decided that she did.

Donovan pulled his hand from his pocket and clutched the Empire pin tightly inside his closed palm. Johnay took notice.

Gray, a burly bear of a teen with a complexion like strong coffee and a jagged scar across one cheek, quickly joined Carr's side as the room divided further. Gray was a bit of an enforcer in Donovan's group and considered most things a fight. His proven bravery and stature carried a lot of weight in Donovan's group.

Gray's family made a hemp-like rope, which was a critical commodity to a society devoid of large machines. Ropes spun of Empire trash and recycled plastics were always in demand for construction hoists and transportation needs. Cordage makers like Gray did well in the Sewers, and that made them a prime target of Black Marketeers and greedy Sewer Rats. It was a good thing Gray liked to fight.

"I agree with Carr," Gray addressed the table. "Trappin' a Rat's nest makes sense." He rubbed his large chin with his equally large paw. "T'was I Boss Dog, I'd wanna know, first off, how big we were, 'n' exactly how dangerous 'fore I moved. Only question now is, how much Black Flag we're into 'n' wot are we gonna do about it?" Grey paused to look over the table. "Might be best t'lay low for a bit. Leave t'nest for a spell."

"Ridiculous." Johnay cut him off. "If by some terrible happenstance t'Empire has even an inkling of our group, why not muster out t'lot of us already. Why let Donnie go in t'first place?" Johnay reasoned. "Beetle-headed Blue Coats had t'book right there in their grasp. They had t'head of the snake. There's barely a dozen of us here. Without our leader, we'd be an easy mark!"

Some of the teens now tapped out agreement and the sands again shifted.

"Wot's it gonna hurt if we hide a bit?" Carr tried to stem the tide.

The room was divided.

Payne, a wild-looking teen with a long thick helmet of jaggedly cut hair, leaned in from the furthest shadows of the table. "I agree with Johnay," Payne began. "But only to a point. I also agree with Carr 'n' Gray.

"So, basically, you have no opinion." Carr dismissed him as the room nervously chuckled.

"Book notwithstanding." he cut her off. "We do now have a far larger 'n' more powerful army than t'Empire knows of, so 'tis likely that they'd need t'know more 'fore making a move 'gainst us. 'Tis certainly worth t'hump of drawin' us outta our hole. T'see how big we are." As the murmurs rose, he cut off the room mid-reaction: "But if we turn tail now, we look guilty. Also, we'd be weaker and more spread out." Then, he eyed Gray. "Our strength comes from our unity. If we divide, who knows who among us might falter at t'sight of enough Empire coin and rock?"

Gray pounded his fist on the table as if the wood was Payne's face. "Who are ye referrin' to, Payne?!?"

"Could be any o' us, Gray!" Payne stood as the room erupted. "We've a cause to protect!"

The room quickly flew into smaller factions and disagreements. Knox had spent the last few minutes listening and pondering all the points. He knew the room was waiting for his take. It was time, so he banged on the table with his fist.

"Hang on a moment! Just hang on!" Slowly, the room came around.

"All of us at this table make salient points." Knox eyed Carr and Gray. "But just how 'xactly would Boss Dog know Donnie was lookin' for t'way out when they scooped him up as an Empire Builder? Why even suspect him, unless they already know from one of us?"

Fear restored a semblance of order to the room, but the fear now included suspicions of each other.

"Are yer eyes not working?" Carr pleaded. "They marked him, Knox." Carr stood from the table and paced away. "They marked 'im, measured 'im, and let'm go right back to t'nest."

"Others got marked," Knox replied almost offhand. He motioned to Crispus. "Crispus is marked."

Crispus nodded in agreement. "Truth." He rubbed his forearm and mark as he followed the logic. "Why not follow me here, then?"

"Because they tossed your knuck carcass outta t'catcher." Carr smirked. "Rejected you outright."

The room managed another nervous chuckle, this time at Crispus's expense, but the teen would have none of it. "I agree with them, Carr." Crispus turned to her. "I got measured when they gave me this." He held up his Empire Builder tattoo. "Been here a hundred times since then t'my family, to visit some o' yours. 'Tis not like they can track us, o' we'd all been mustered out."

The point stopped Carr's momentum and she hovered back near her seat.

Donovan caught himself squeezing the Empire pin. He was thinking about where he'd throw it away.

"Boss Dog watches a lot more than y'think." Gray placed two large, battered, and calloused hands on the table. "Sewers are full'a

turncoats an' Empire Mules. I got 'em crawlin' around constant."
He eyed Payne. "But Payne's right, too. This very room is a Black-
Flag assembly. Any one o' us could make a pretty rock turnin' us
all in. Boss Dog is just waitin' for t'right time. I can feel the neck
twine tightenin' as we speak, so all I'm suggestin' 'tis this." Gray
took a moment to measure the words. "Might it not be such a bad
turn t'pull back for a bit, that's all." He looked around the table.
"Spell a few weeks 'til things quiet down. We can use my family's
cordage cellar to hold our meetings."

A few of the teens began to bang on the table in a show of
support for Gray's plan.

"Boss Dog's money comes from the Colonies," Knox interrupted the display. "Their cheap and slave labor comes from us.
It's a perfect system, really. We have no power, 'cept in this room,
maybe. Your cordage enterprise aside," he eyed Gray, "Rats are not
worth t'lead to put them down."

"But wot about revolutionaries?" Crispus stopped the room.

Several of the teens again began to pound the table. In a few
moments, the room was spiraling out of control again and split-
ting into factions.

Johnay shot Donovan a cool smile. He liked to push his leader's buttons. In as much as Johnay didn't want the responsibility of
being in charge, he positively thrived on pulling strings. He knew
Donovan was hiding something and holding back. He wanted his
leader to lead the cause.

"Got yourself into t'thick o' it now," Johnay prodded him as
the room argued back and forth.

"Me?"

Johnay nodded.

"You've a better idea?" Donovan smirked back.

"With our necks a few inches from t'rope, t'least you might offer would be t'whole truth o' it."

"He'd have to get that boot from his mush first," Knox chided as he eavesdropped.

Behind the conversation, Carr and Gray made their point to abandon the Dogue Run home.

"Havin' both boots for use would make the next step a fair bit easier," Knox needled Donovan further.

"Fear," Johnay's look became serious as he took a poised breath, "must never be t'foundation o' leadership. Let it not be that foundation now."

Even in the midst of the chaos, the comment made Donovan smile. Johnay always had a knack for cutting to the heart of things. The three teens formed a great group—Donovan the idealist, Johnay the deep thinker, and Knox the strategist.

"So, can you tell us t'rest o' it and get on with things?" Johnay prodded him now. "'N' don't dump t'manure cart on me either." Johnay ran his fingers through his red hair casually. "I know when you think you're protecting us from something else."

The inference took hold of the room and gradually, even as they argued, a sea of impatient eyes glanced Donovan's way.

"Wish I knew how t'protect myself from you." Donovan fixed Johnay in a narrow stare.

"Impossible." Johnay grinned back.

Donovan then turned back to the room. They were ready to take a vote on hiding out in Gray's cordage cellar.

"'Tis 'nother consideration," Donovan shouted over the din before pounding his fists on the table. "'TIS ANOTHER WAY!"

The room slowly settled. Johnay winked at Knox as if to suggest that he really controlled the room.

"That is?" Gray finally challenged the Dogue Run leader.

"We can leave t'Sewers."

Carr blinked. The room hushed.

Donovan followed his statement with a definitive period. "If I'm indeed target of Boss Dog's treachery, I can make t'lot o' you safe by goin'." He smiled. "Or, we can all go."

Johnay's eyes widened. This was not the moment he was trying to orchestrate. "Go? Go where?" he stammered.

"The Colonies."

Silence. Carr sat down. She felt safer now, yet somehow completely vulnerable.

"B'fore I was picked up by t'Empire Builder transport," Donovan paced back to the "Freedom or Death" slogan on the wall, where he eyed Johnay and Knox. Here came the truth. "I skulked off to Perimeter Five."

The news shocked the entire assembly.

"You wot?" Carr's eyes widened. "You went Black Flag and then came back here?" Carr shuddered. The room followed her lead.

"I found t'way out, Carr." Donovan eyed the room. It was still his for the moment, but the Empire pin weighed heavy in his fingers.

Crispus was confused. "But y'sed y'got picked up as a Builder off Auld Way?"

"Donnie?" Knox pressed. "Wot happened in Perimeter Five?"

The room waited on Donovan. It was a short leash.

"Un'er t'Empire in Perimeter Five," Donovan took a breath, "I found t'Constable's Keep."

"'N' a way to the Empire?" Grey asked hopefully.

Donovan just shook his head and watched the reaction from the divided room. For effect, he waited for the room to heat up before slamming his father's book onto the map on the table. "I found my father!" he finally thundered. "Dr. Princeton Rush."

The room stopped cold.

"Brothers and Sisters o' the Sword," Donovan spat the phrase derisively as he turned away from the table. "A lovely little trifle o' a name for wot we profess t'stand for." Donovan spun back. "Rats are not worth t'lead t'put them down, y'say." He eyed Knox. "Barely a dozen o' us, wot can we do?" Donovan put his hands on Johnay's shoulders. "Divided t'lot o' us, like the blasted Dogue Run Council was." He let the statement sink in. "Rats on a sinkin' ship," he pushed again until he knew some in the room were taking offense. "I put it forth that we're not simply rats 'n' we're certainly not just a dozen."

He then paced all the way around the table again and stopped in front of the "Freedom or Death" slogan. "M'father taught that t'Sewers were t'orginal Empire." He exhaled. "My father ne'er understood wot divided us. I don't understand now. He used t'talk about how we as a people allowed ourselves t'be divided, by money 'n' by class, birth, 'n' rank. He talked o' a time early in t'Empire when t'wasn't so. We once had a plan he wrote, to equalize t'power so that no group could own advantage o'er 'nother. In t'original Empire, he said, we were meant to be accountable to our brothers 'n' sisters, to all own a bit o' t'Empire, somethin' t'protect t'gether. Somethin' we had a sacred right to." Donovan paced completely around the group.

"Today, we don't even own our Sewer; t'property rights o' those above extend below. This entire place," he spread his arms out, "'tis owned by t'Imperial Zoo and Park above our heads." He pointed to Knox. "Knox here says Boss Dog changed t'history books, too, t'hide our past. This way, only people who were none older than a grandparent might e'er remember a scrap or trifle. Empire knows most o' all that wot you don't know, you can't b'lieve, but that's wot b'lief is 'sposed to be—t'b'lief in somethin' better that doesn't yet exist or hasn't yet been created." He paused again. "Or can only be proved by test."

Some of the teens began to bang on the table in support of Donovan's words. He raised a hand to stop them. He wasn't done. "E'en as m'brother Knox here points out when he speaks of how t'Rats, t'Colonies, and t'Empire all fit t'gether, it's like a trio of trading partners, each takin' mo advantage o'er t'next, more like a trio o' countries than o' classes and properties."

Donovan then strolled over to Carr and Gray. "Carr and Gray here are spot on as well." He looked over the rest of the group as Carr and Gray exchanged a look. "Were I Boss Dog, I'd be drawin' us out too…hopin' we run from our ship." Donovan waited for the right moment to pace back to the slogan. "But we're not rats, we're not ideas. We're not just a dozen souls." He raised his voice: "'N' THIS PLACE 'TISN'T A BLASTED SEWER! 'TIS A COUNTRY O' ITS OWN!"

Eyes lit up around the table as the candlelight and ideas filled them. "And in times o' crisis, some may shrink fro' t'service to one's country." He was winning the room and he knew it. "'Tis the business of little minds t'shrink." He screwed a steely smile onto his face. "But those whose hearts are firm, and whose conscience approves their conduct, will pursue their principles unto death." As the room fell silent in his grasp, Donovan lowered his voice to a whisper. "Freedom or death."

The culmination of Donovan's speech was met by a storm of fists pounding the table. He managed a wink at Johnay, but Gray, ever the troublemaker, still had some trouble to make. He held his two hands up like an act of surrender and turned to Donovan.

"Hang on, hang on!" He waited for the room to settle. "You said you found your old man?" He eyed Donovan and cocked his head to one side. "In the Keep?"

Confusion crept across the table.

"Wot o' it?" Donovan tried to defend his moment.

Crispus verbalized what the others were suddenly thinking. "Rotting in the Keep is hardly out, Donnie."

All eyes turned to Donovan.

"'Fore that, he made it all the way to t'Empire, Crispus."

"So you say." Carr's eyes narrowed. The room seemed to teeter all at once.

Donovan opened the book to what everybody could see was a whole new map written in the hand of his father. He then smiled and thumped his hand down on it. Carr and Gray had bumbled right into his setup. Knox, ever the strategist, gave Donovan a respectful nod. The teen leader had set a fine trap.

"Added this t'his own book, by his own hand." Donovan's confidence lit the room. "An' he stayed b'hind so Boss Dog wouldn't find out our plans."

Donovan then shoved the book in front of Carr and Gray. Their eyes opened wider as they checked against the previous maps; it was indeed the same hand. The book then passed from new hand to new hand, wide eyes to wide eyes, fueling a focused excitement as it did. Donovan waited for it to get full circle and then spread his hands out on the map that was painted on the table.

"He said t'filtration gates are t'way out." Donovan tapped his fingers on the appropriate place on the map. "Right here in Fairfax Flats. Said he left it out o' t'book to protect us." Donovan grabbed the book and held it up in the flickering light and pointed to the gates, the Channel, and the goal. "There 'tis! Rhodes Colony. That's t'way! 'Tis wot we drilled for, 'tis e'rything we planned for!"

"A way into leg irons, the lash mast, or the hangman's noose," was Carr's last gasp of fear and defiance. "We'll be mustered out or marked for this."

"Wot are we now!?!" Donovan snapped. "Ev'n if we don't make it, others will follow just 'cause we tried. We do this for t'children that come af'er us. If that be not t'noblest of cause, wot is?"

The room again erupted in support. Carr watched incredulously as Gray joined the group.

"How we supposed to get past the gates?" Payne leaned over the map.

"When they lifted me up in t'Empire Transport," Donovan pointedly met each and every eye at the table, "I saw t'path, catwalks and such, wot Boss Dog's Sewer Guard uses t'fix things."

"T'gates and those walks are patrolled. Sewer Guards'll kill us for the coin! It won't work," Carr tried again.

"I can find t'way to the Militia Guard positions through my contacts," Knox assured the Brothers and Sisters of the Sword. "Not all o' them are as loyal as Boss Dog thinks."

"Aye. Spreadin' some coin should help…" Payne reasoned.

"If it's coin you need, it's coin I got," Gray chimed in now.

After a beat, the stunned room suddenly erupted in singular support. The seed had been planted; the spirit was rising. Not even Carr's glare towards Gray could slow it now. "Dyin' in t'Channel or t'Colonies sure seems a better fate than here in t'Sewers." He shrugged to Carr.

"I can get us some maintenance flatboats," Knox shouted into the ruckus. "We can disguise ourselves as a Militia crew."

Donovan walked to the "Freedom or Death" logo. "We sail fo' the Rhodes Colony, then," he shouted to cheers and fist bangs.

"We take root there…blend in an' organize…establish a base… we grow a tree o' liberty! We find a way out fo' more o' our kind! FREEDOM OR DEATH!"

The room exploded into cheers. "FREEDOM OR DEATH! FREEDOM OR DEATH!"

Two of the Sentry guards opened the blackened window and peered in. What they saw made them smile.

Johnay looked up at Donovan warily. "You know this is gonna start a bloody war."

"Let it start, Johnay," Donovan said inwardly. "Let it start."

6

A SECOND CROSSING

MILES ABOVE AND AWAY, the sprawling Magistrate Tower glistened against the night sky, seemingly as indifferent to the Sewers beneath as its surroundings. In some respects, the very seat of Imperial government seemed to possess no particular reason for being, aside from that the march of time and nature had made it so. Still, high up at one end of the sprawling arch that spanned the crown's apex, a lone figure stood in a lit window. Though rendered charcoal-gray in the dim light, Dr. Franklin's silhouette was as plain as the mostly white office behind him.

There, a grand fireplace sat at one end of a large and open space. Near the center, a simple white wooden desk and chair stood as if taking up a safe distance from the fire. All around, towering office windows framed the city below like ever-changing works of art. It was the only decoration that Franklin allowed, the view outside. Throughout his career, Richard Franklin had always been a practical man, devoid of creature comforts and the trappings of affluence and power. He considered himself a servant of the world, an attitude that had brought him much influence and power within the Empire. Still, he often wondered why his humble life lessons were never taken as an example but rather used as a resource. The strange juxtaposition bonded him with the Colonies and Sewers. It also bonded him with his friend Dr. Rush, the man he made sure got a Keep prison cell rather than a hemp necktie. It now also bonded him with Donovan Washington Rush. The Empire above, like the Sewers below, suddenly had a glimmer of hope that things could change.

Franklin looked down at Empire City and just how far below the people were from his and His Magistrate's tower. *Money and power*, he thought, *has never made one happy, nor will it. There is nothing in its nature to produce happiness. The more of it one has, the more one wants.* Franklin rubbed the thought into his prominent chin and paced back to his desk. His tablet was waiting for him alongside his digital quill. He flopped back the tails on his coat and sat. Dr. Franklin loved to think about the people. He loved to write.

A Recipe for Losing an Empire (or losing a cake)

Consider that a great empire, like a great cake, is most easily diminished at the edges. Turn your attention, therefore, first to your remotest provinces so that as you get rid of them, the next may follow in order.

For the possibility of this separation to always exist, take special care that the provinces are never incorporated with the mother country—that they do not enjoy the same common rights, the same privileges in commerce, and that they are governed by severer laws without allowing them any share in the choice of the legislators.

By carefully making and preserving such distinctions, you will (to keep to my simile of the cake) act like a wise gingerbread baker, who, to facilitate a division, cuts his dough half through in those places where, when baked, he would have it broken to pieces.

Those remote provinces have perhaps been acquired, purchased, or conquered, at the sole expense of the settlers or their ancestors without the aid of the mother country. If this should happen to increase her strength, by their growing numbers, ready to join in her wars; her commerce, by their growing demand for her manufactures; or her military power, by greater employment for her soldiers and law enforcers, they may probably suppose some merit in this, and that it entitles them to some favor; you are therefore to forget it all or resent it, as if they had done you injury.

If they happen to be zealous friends of liberty, nurtured in revolution principles, remember all that to their prejudice, and resolve to punish it, for such principles, after a revolution is thoroughly established, are of no more use; they are even odious and abominable.

However peaceably your colonies have submitted to your government, shewn their affection to your interests, and patiently borne their grievances, you are to suppose them always inclined to revolt and treat them accordingly. Quarter troops among them, who by their insolence may provoke the rising of mobs, and by their bullets and bayonets suppress them. By this means, like the husband who uses his *wife ill from suspicion, you may in time convert your suspicions into realities.*

Franklin's stylus pen and words cut like a surgeon's blade as they flew at a frenzied pace, probing the opened heart of his own Empire. At a most delicate phase of his operation, he suddenly stopped. There was a lone figure standing at his door, tall, broad, and a military type in a long blue coat and gold sash. He held his three-seed hat under his arm in a gesture of polite respect. A general.

"Dr. Franklin?" General John Goynes peered at the dimly lit silhouette in the center of the room. "Does His Magistrate always prefer you kept in the dark thusly?"

Though his body just an outline, Franklin could see the smile on Goynes's face and chuckled as the general approached. He knew Goynes well enough from social circles, well enough to jab back at the thinly veiled gloat.

"Darkness is best suited to soldiers I think." Franklin smirked. "You are natural skulkers and sneakers. Under cover of darkness, as it were."

Goynes tried to spy a glimpse of Franklin's tablet and what had occupied him so. He was even more amused when it appeared that Franklin turned it away from his prying eyes.

"Another of your subversive books?" He flashed a sly grin.

"I thought His Magistrate rather fancied my writing." Franklin's expression sank into mock offense and hurt.

"Until he sees my next play." Goynes winked and then paced away towards the windows. "A sweeping and utterly dramatic tale of a renowned government minister fomenting a Shakespearean revolt in the halls of empire." Goynes then spun back with a smile, his long coat dramatically flowing just behind his turn.

Franklin set his tablet down on the desk and laughed. He played to the room as if on stage. "Empire, hear me. Beware the dramatist soldier, whose words do more damage than his men ever have."

Goynes bowed playfully, clasping and swinging his hat before returning to the desk where Franklin stood. There, he eyed his friend playfully. "One can do nothing in the Empire without celebrity, Richard. Surely you, after all of your books and lectures, know this."

"I rather fancy myself more of a scientist, John." Franklin raised an eyebrow. "A social engineer." He paused. "Celebrity sounds so..." he paused again. "Shallow."

"We have engineers in the military too," Goynes gently nudged Franklin as he smoothed out his golden military sash in a casual display of rank. "And celebrities." His eyes sparkled. "Neither make good soldiers."

Franklin chuckled. "Why are you here so late, anyway? Are we attacking somebody?"

Goynes smirked through a sigh. "Not yet."

"Oh?"

"But I did have matters of import to discuss with His Magistrate."

"Such as?"

Goynes took a breath. "I am investigating some improprieties in the Bay's Colonial Council."

"That of Governor Shirley." Franklin nodded. He knew him well.

"One and the same." Goynes seemed buoyant from his assignment.

"So, only now does the Empire get around to looking into old news?"

"Yes." Goynes nodded. "Because it's far more than usual. There has been a marked increase in imports from our friends the Capes."

"Oh? What's the nature of the issue?" Franklin's curiosity was piqued.

"It seems some Cape merchants and merchant exporters have been using their low tariffs to bring in electronics goods from Huaxia at a vast discount and then, with certain factions of Colonial assistance, fixing prices to profiteer off the Empire."

"Trade with Huaxia is restricted," Franklin noted the obvious. "Many in these halls consider them our enemy."

Goynes eyed him. "Tell that to the Capes, and while you are at it, to the Governors of Rhodes, Conn's, Trent, and Penn's."

Franklin pondered the Capes, one of the Empire's oldest historical foes, though a powerful potential ally. "This sounds like a dangerous affair," he remarked.

Goynes nodded inwardly as he thought of the opportunity before him. "One could only hope so."

Franklin watched the general's reaction closely before continuing. "Who came up with such a cockeyed scheme?"

General Goynes shifted on his feet. "What is a well-spent life but a series of chances taken?"

"This was your idea, was it not?" Franklin smiled as he gently admonished his friend. "You know, John. It takes many good deeds to build a good reputation, and only one bad one to lose it." Franklin chuckled and paced away to the window. "How are you ever going to escape this life of military servitude if you don't cease your constant missions and causes?"

"Perhaps like you so often claim in your collected literary works, I was simply born to serve."

Franklin turned, his face suddenly full of mischief and sport. He bowed at the well-placed jab.

"Are we so different, Richard?" Goynes joined Franklin at the window. "I collect military titles and promotions. You collect what? Daughters and sisters of aristocracy?"

Both men shared a smile at Franklin's vast and not-so-secret list of liaisons and dalliances. "We are both, it seems, attracted to conquest. I simply fancy mine of a more lasting nature," Goynes mused.

"You just hang around with the wrong women, John." Franklin smirked before pacing away. "This investigation sounds rather bleak by comparison." Franklin playfully looked down. "Even for a writer."

Goynes sighed. "It's not very popular, I must tell you."

"Does this illicit activity in the Colonies still benefit the Empire?"

"Mostly." Goynes nodded.

Franklin turned back for his desk. "Good luck, then. Once you get far enough in your investigation that you are required to look up at those you suspect, be sure to watch your own neck lest someone slip a rope around it!"

Goynes laughed. Franklin's tablet suddenly flashed to life; a map sprung up on the screen before it was covered over by a security access prompt. Goynes only caught a glimpse and Franklin quickly picked it up.

"An urgent call?" Goynes eyed him a beat. It seemed off to him.

"Something like that," Franklin downplayed.

"Well." The general bowed. "I'll leave you to your mistresses and, for the time being, I shall attend to mine."

As Goynes strutted for the door, Franklin unlocked the device. On the map, the Empire pin signal designated DWR for Donovan

Washington Rush was on the move in the Fairfax Sewers. It was on the move in the maintenance canals and towards the forbidden waste gates of Fairfax Flats. The image of the moving Empire pin sparkled in Franklin's eyes.

Before he vanished into the halls, General Goynes stopped in the door to watch. When Franklin sensed the presence and looked up, Goynes was gone.

The Sewer maintenance canals looked like a dark and dirty mix of purgatory and coastal ruin, filled with dank hazy air, the foul smoke from trash fires, and the steam of hot wastewater that spewed from under Fairfax Flats. It was a toxic brew of abject poverty and utter despair. Amidst the narrow Channel, debris-strewn waterways, and broken-down landings and walkways, a small boat made of patchwork metal and wood moved through the haze. The small flat craft was crowded with eight dirty and well-armed teens, among them Donovan, Carr, Crispus, Johnay, and Gray. Four other boats trailed, but missing from the assembly group of running Rats were Payne and Knox.

The maintenance flatboat was dug out in the middle where most of the teens huddled. There was one teen pilot at the bow and two at the stern. They dipped long poles into the brackish water to maneuver the boat. Donovan stood up front too, his long coat thrown over his shoulders like a cape.

As the group neared the massive filtration gates that kept the worst of the sewage out of the Channel, Colonies, and Empire, a putrid wind began to kick up. It lifted Donovan's coat like a battle flag.

Johnay came to his leader's side and braced against the foul breeze. "And I thought *we* smelled awful," he joked.

"That's not us, Johnay, 'tis t'Empire."

As the distant shadows of the massive filtration gates loomed larger, the breeze became cold and thicker still with the odor of decay. "Smells like death just t'same." Johnay shuddered as he pulled his collar closer.

"I expect a lot o' us'll be mustered out by midnight," Donovan observed. The words were said quietly and meant only for Johnay. He wasn't happy to hear them.

Crispus was close enough to catch it. "Not if'n we can vanish into the dirt 'n' shadow b'fore the Lawbrokers 'n' the Colonial Council knows we're there," he offered as he placed a lean hand on Johnay's shoulder.

Johnay took kindly to the words even if he had no faith in them. Gallows humor ruled the moment. "Show me one useless bastard, that's a shame." Johnay forced a smile and turned to the rest of the boat. "Show me two...that's a Lawbroker patrol; show me a bunch of useless bastards, I'll show you a Colonial Council."

The group shared a nervous laugh as up ahead in the steam and mist, a giant dark maw opened before them. Slowly, the filthy and rusted five-story-tall metal filtration gate emerged from the haze. It was certainly designed to filter the water as best as possible before it escaped into the Channel, but more so, it was meant to keep anything inside from getting out.

From a vantage point high above, the small flotilla of flatboats announced themselves by the sound of their steering poles cutting the shallow water. Leaning in to watch was a band of five Sewer guards with their tattered coats, crown armbands, and combat helmets. As unpleasant as Sewer Guard patrol was, it meant continued survival and, possibly, money.

A brash teen named White, small for a Sewer Guard, stood out from his teen army in voice and demeanor. He quickly stepped forward and issued his command. "Turn out! Main Guard! Irons at the ready!"

Five Barking Irons quickly extended into rifle mode and were trained on Donovan's lead boat.

Down in the maintenance canal, Carr thought she spied movement in the shadows high above. She grabbed Crispus by the arm and pointed. Soon, Donovan, Johnay, and Crispus were all looking up. Donovan motioned to the back of his flatboat where two of the Dogue Run sentries were stationed with their boom sticks. He pointed and they took aim.

"Pass word t'the other boats," Donovan whispered. "Stand ready."

Carr nodded silently and went aft. She grabbed a small signal lamp and began to flash instructions to the other boats.

The next few moments passed without incident. The shadows above seemed empty, but the ones just ahead were not.

"Where in t'hell do y'think you knucks are going?" Sewer Guard Captain White shouted down from straight above Donovan's boat. "Private Catawba, ready to fire!" White directed his lead gunner, a caramel-hued teen with long hair pulled into a high ponytail.

Guns then readied on both sides, and with five more sentries on the boats behind Donovan's, it became a deadly standoff.

"Lot further than a bloody turncoat Empire Mule like you." Donovan stood tall at the bow.

High above on the hidden catwalks, Captain White stepped into the light. "Boys?" He leaned to his assembled men. "Looks like we all be fetchin' some shiny new coin with these dead carcasses." Ominous laughs rose from the hidden ranks. "Boxman's gonna be busy tonight." More laughs entered the mist and echoed like ghosts yet to come.

With all eyes upon him, Donovan was unbowed, yet strangely held out his hand behind him, motioning for his troops not to fire.

"A few scraps maybe," Donovan defied the Sewer guard. "Fine wage for someone's property guarding more o' the same Boss Dog's property."

"Wot's that?" Captain White was incredulous. "At least I'm worth something." He used his anger to collect himself. "You Rats 'r' worth more dead than alive."

Between his fingers, Donovan nervously rolled the Empire pin like a poker chip. The Sewer guard had the clear advantage and Donovan wondered if he'd indeed just bet far over his head.

"If y'let us pass," he stalled, "maybe we're gonna change a few things...for all o' us Rats."

Captain White turned to his men and shook his head. Then, he walked to the edge of the catwalk, folded his arms, and looked straight down at Donovan.

"'Tis that so? Wot's yer name, Rat?"

"Donovan Washington Rush, sir." Donovan held up his arm and his tattoo. "Empire Builder."

"Here now." White hesitated. "How'd y'get back to the Sewer with that?" He glanced back at his men with a smirk. "Were y'rejected?"

His men laughed some more. Donovan just stared back.

"I did my service and they sent me back," Donovan told the truth.

It gave White pause, if only for a moment. He had his sights on money and power. The truth was the last thing on his mind. "Sewer Rats ain't allowed t'assemble, and it's Black Flag t'organize," he towed the Empire line.

Donovan's stoic silence caused White's tone to darken considerably.

"Besides, wot are the straggly band of you gonna do against the Empire? Start a bloody revolution?" White suddenly burst out laughing at the thought. His fellow guards quickly joined in.

"We could use a militia," Donovan challenged White again.

The statement produced even more howls of laughter. "I wager you could right 'bout now!"

Everybody on Donovan's boat and the ones behind began to wonder if this was truly the end of their rope. Donovan just smiled as a half dozen Sewer Rats led by Knox and Payne came up behind White and his men. White's Sewer Guard noticed too late and, in the darkened shadows, were quickly subdued. Some were grabbed and shoved to their knees at the end of blades, others rendered silent by boom sticks stuck into their wide-eyed faces. The only two who dared resist were nearly crushed together between Knox's bear paws.

The cocky Captain White was especially taken by surprise, not readily noticing the sounds of commotion behind him until they echoed against the filtration gate and reverberated all the way down to Donovan's boats below. Suddenly resigned, White slowly lowered his weapon and tensed as equally inky shapes emerged from the dirty shadows behind him. He'd been had.

As Payne leaned in to take White's weapon, he smiled. "See?" He loudly called down to the boats below. "Things are changin' already."

The entire mass of Donovan's boats was stunned to silence. Their plan had worked. In seconds, they let loose an explosion of relief and joy. "BOOYAH! BOOYAH!" Followed by "FREEDOM OR DEATH!"

It took a moment for White to screw up the courage to fully survey his failure. There in the center of it, Knox stared back, the worst possible turn. Knox was once a fellow Sewer Guard, now a Black-Flag Sewer turncoat.

"You'll hang fo' this, Mr. Knox," White seethed.

Knox just smiled. "It'll take a lot o' rope, Mr. White. Lot more than you got." Knox then pressed the barrel of his boom stick into White's temple. "Open the gate!" White was frozen.

Shoved aside and relieved of his boom stick, Private Catawba edged closer. He was more captivated than fearful. He was from the land in the Sewers that Tarleton had mentioned called HillsLand, where many other Rats spoke of rebellion and unity against the Empire. It was a dream that Catawba had given up on years prior, yet here it was again, and right before him. In Captain White's hesitation, Private Catawba recovered this long-lost purpose and stepped silently to the filtration gate controls. A moment later, the Fairfax Flats filtration gate screamed in violation as it ground open. Hundreds of years of dirt, rust, and ancient patina fell away and a gale of wind flew in, knocking Donovan's boats sideways. His long coat-turned-cape billowed behind him as he pointed ahead.

"TO RHODES!" he screamed.

As his crew cheered him on. Carr, Johnay, Gray, and Crispus took in the sight as the massive gate door opened to a horizon of water, Donovan Washington Rush standing before it, captain of a ship, captain of their every hope.

As the convoy of flatboats disappeared out into the two-hundred-mile-wide Channel, Payne, Knox, and their party finished disarming the Sewer Guard and began to withdraw.

"When I tell Boss Dog…" White blustered a new threat.

"You won't tell a soul," Payne cut him off. "First neck t'stretch'll be your own."

Payne was right. "If y'don't speak o' it," he smiled tauntingly, "neither will I."

In a moment, Payne, Knox, and their small party was gone into the shadows. White's men quickly assembled and, before any of them could speak, he had new orders.

"Let 'em run," he growled. "Leave 'em to t'Colonials. Only thing findin' t'shore'll be their blood." Catawba stepped to the edge of the catwalk to watch as Donovan and party vanished into a merging of black water and sky. He secretly wished them well.

A few moments later, as Donovan's convoy crossed the threshold into the Channel, the huge gate slammed closed behind them.

Death's a doorway. Donovan thought about his father's words. This time, he smiled. Donovan the Sewer Rat was dead. Donovan the Colonial was about to be born.

7

TWO SHIPS

Dr. Franklin sat transfixed at his desk, stunned even, as he watched the tiny blip of Donovan Washington Rush pass beyond the border of the Sewer and out into the Channel. The soft light of the tablet washed over Franklin's face as his eyes darted back and forth on the map. In the darkness of his office in the Magistrate's Tower, Franklin smiled.

"Good lad," he marveled. "Freedom's not given; it's taken."

More than five hundred miles away, Donovan's armada plowed its way through the icy waters as trash, small chunks of ice, debris, and even what looked like discarded and decaying body parts bumped back at them. Donovan hid his impression of it all. *Is this a sign of things to come?*

Slowly, above, the low mist and clouds parted, and a sparkling canopy of stars filled the void. Carr had never seen anything like it in her life.

"Wot in t'Lord's good name is that?" Her heart rose into her throat as tears descended her cheeks.

"It's the sky, Carr." Donovan turned to her.

"And those lights," Gray was breathless, "are stars?"

"That's t'difference between us and t'Empire, Gray," Donovan observed poetically. "Whereas they look down and see those like us at their feet, we look up and see past them all to the stars beyond."

Johnay couldn't resist the opportunity to call him out. "You read far too much, Donnie."

"One o' us better," Donovan huffed. "O' there'd be no more need for writers."

High up in the Magistrate's Tower, Dr. Franklin was marking the moment in his favorite way—by writing about it.

I traveled much in my youth, and I observed in different countries and our own colonies that the more public provisions were made for the poor, the less they provided for themselves and, of course, became poorer. And, on the contrary, the less was done for them outside of increased opportunities, the more they did for themselves, and became richer. I am for doing good to the poor, but I differ in opinion of the means. I think the best way of doing good to the poor is not by making life easy in poverty but by leading or driving them out of it.

Ahead of Donovan's convoy, faint orange and yellow lights came into view. The closer they edged their boats to the lights, the more of them became visible. Soon, flickering dots of colors spread out as far as the eye could see. Every teen clambered to the front of their boat to look. The Colonies looked endless; they looked free.

A thousand yards ahead, scores of flat panel displays blared out from the wooden and stone buildings all over the NewTown Coast. Unlike the Empire above and Sewers below, where such displays were scarce except for the occasional official Imperial Proclamation Board, the Colony streets and buildings were covered in advertisements of every kind. The endless barrage of digital color washed the shadows, buildings, and cobblestones into a perpetual pastel dusk.

Across Thames Street and near the warehouses foretold by Dr. Rush, human shapes moved in the shadows above a large customs house. Below in a dark alley, a tiny blue light flashed. At the end of the same alley, perched atop her later-model electric motorcycle, was KZ Fayette, the gang leader that Lawbroker Cruz had chased three years prior, leading to the terrible accident that killed a mother and child.

KZ had risen far in the ranks since that night. She was now the head of a black-market gang known as "The Prophets" and was not only involved in the Capes and Huaxia plot to fix prices and profiteer that General Goynes wished to stop, but she was one of the leaders. KZ was wiry and slight, but like a cobra, all dangerous beauty, coiled muscle, and venom.

Behind her, several more teens on bikes assembled next to an old banged-up charcoal-gray panel truck. She waited a few beats as another red light winked from the darkness ahead, a courtyard of sorts in the midst of the customs house. She used a penlight slung from her wrist to flash back a single blue burst and then powered up her bike.

"Make tracks." She nodded to her gang and moved out slowly ahead of them, leading her group into the customs house courtyard where they killed the lights on their bikes and coasted to a stop. KZ then flipped open a mobile phone of sorts, something never seen in the Sewers, and dialed a number. The grim face of a surly male teen popped up before her. It was her lieutenant, Mense.

"On station," Mense reported in what KZ knew as his usual detached manner.

KZ killed her phone without a word or a nod and waited. After a minute, another group of bikes entered the courtyard on the opposite side. They, too, were accompanied by a panel truck. This one was black and covered in Colonial graffiti.

KZ waited for the scene to settle, then calmly dismounted her bike and walked to the center of the yard. A few in her crew dismounted behind her and took out their weapons, far more sophisticated versions of the Sewer boom sticks.

Crank, a hollow-faced twenty-something colorfully dressed and with a streak of gold painted through his hair, headed up the other faction. KZ knew Crank well enough to not trust him for a second. Crank arrived at the center of the courtyard first and waited. The look on his face seemed like the entire meeting was a huge ordeal. As KZ approached, Crank milked the moment by checking his watch, folding his arms, and screwing a bony frown across his dirty face. A few menacing guards stepped out beside him. KZ barely blinked as she walked over to meet him.

"Figure the longer I sit on this stuff," Crank mused to his own crowd, "the price'll just keep going up. Why don't y'come back next week, when supplies are short and I can really stick ya?"

One of KZ's party tensed at his gun; one of Crank's followed suit.

"Turncoat profiteer," the teen to KZ's left muttered above his twitching trigger finger.

KZ reached out her hand and placed it on her man's shoulder to stop and steady him. Then, with her other hand, she gently rubbed a Hanzi-style medallion that hung around her neck.

"Need a little luck tonight, love?" Crank teased.

"You know, Cranky," KZ smiled deceptively under an intense stare, "if my crew blows your shipment all to hell, it won't be worth a rock...and you'll be on the hook with the Colonial Council for it."

"What's it to you?" Crank seethed with indignation. "Since when are you the patriot?"

"I'm not," KZ stared back. "You and your Council cronies wanna knuck from the Empire, that's your business, but when you try and knuck from me and put me on the hook with you, that's another story entirely."

Crank's guards tensed. KZ's crew responded. The situation was escalating quickly.

"I could take the lot of you down," Crank growled. "Claim you were tryin' to break into customs."

"Colonial necks or yours." KZ ignored the bluster and shrugged indifferently.

Crank just shook his head and smiled away his growing anger. "The famous Kai Zi...the holy woman knuck...well, the deal's over m'lady.... I got friends in high places, too."

Crank abruptly turned and motioned to his men to pull back. POP! POP! POP! Shots from above hit the dirt at his feet. His men tensed to fire but, not knowing exactly where the shots came from, quickly realized they were set up. Just as they trained their weapons on KZ and her crew and clicked their rifles into firing position, a star-field of blue lights lit up above and around them.

KZ smiled. The entire courtyard was surrounded by her gang. Mense had stationed them all around the roof of the customs house.

"Looks as if my high up friends are here, Cranky." KZ smirked coldly. "Where are the lot of yours, I wonder?"

Crank seethed as he exchanged looks with his two closest men. "You just made yourself a bigger target."

"I don't think that at all." She motioned her gang forward to Crank's truck. "All I've done is to secure our trade for the price negotiated." She began to turn away but then suddenly stopped. "And," she brought her hand to her face and rubbed her lower lip seductively, "I might have just saved your neck for you."

"Here now?" Crank protested.

"There's talk of an Empire investigation comin' down."

Crank's eyes widened.

"Best keep those eyes open." She smiled as she patted his cheek. "Lawbrokers are watching."

"I own those Lawbrokers, KZ, more than you." Even Crank didn't fully believe his words.

KZ calmly strolled away to the truck.

One of Crank's men turned to him with a rage-filled glare, a silent look that asked, "Aren't you going to do something?"

"Not tonight." Crank pushed past his men. "Tomorrow's another day." Crank then walked back to his bike and climbed on. He motioned for his men to pull back to their bikes just as KZ's group finished up transferring the cargo from Crank's truck to hers. Peering into the truck, KZ scanned the boxes and crates of electronics parts, all bearing the mark of Huaxia, one of the Empire's restricted trading partners, but one whose goods were always in high demand. Even though KZ's loyalties were to her father's Huaxia more than her mother's Capes, she preferred to balance the two for the benefit of both Empire and her pockets. KZ fancied herself a forward-thinker, a girl that someday might change the business world.

After a couple more minutes, it was done and Crank and his gang were on the move. As soon as the courtyard was clear, Mense used a drainpipe to skillfully slide down from his high perch.

"Made a tidy profit tonight." He slid close to KZ's side.

She pulled away an inch.

"Could have been more." He reached for her hair and she stopped him.

"For who?" She eyed him. There was chemistry, but she was having none of it. "We're just a bunch of small-time knucks under a dung heap of knucks tryin' to find a balance. That's the only way to survive in this dump, Mense, until we can move up."

Mense tensed and looked off into the docks where the last of Crank's bikes vanished into Thames Street. "What if Crank really has friends up high, like he says?"

KZ shook off the question as she walked to her bike. "Some on the Council might be greedy and beetle-headed enough to get mixed up with Rhodes Colonial gangs, but they're not stupid enough to stick their necks out for the likes o'them." Then she chuckled. "Not at these margins, anyway!"

Mense followed. "So, they're not gonna stick 'em out for us either if the whole powder keg goes."

KZ knew Mense was spot-on. They were skirting a tenuous line with no clear allies on either side of it. KZ climbed onto her bike and switched it on, then turned back to him. "Exactly why we're not gonna push it—not with this investigation hangin' about."

Mense nodded and looked out towards the waterfront. "Sounds like a fool's errand," he mused. "Some kinda Empire Mule lookin' to make a fuss and muscle in on our coin." Something out in the water caught his eye. He stopped.

Out in the Channel, Donovan watched the back of his flatboat, where two boatsmen carefully pushed and dragged their quant poles into the water to nudge and steer the ship towards the shore. *Like entering the Colonies themselves*, Donovan thought. *Push too hard or drag too much and we'll all sink.* All around them, low foggy clouds clung to the water like a vast layer of perpetually kicked-up dust. The lights of the Colonies barely flickered through, and though they spread out towards the horizon in both directions, it was impossible to discern how near or how far.

"Shallowing, Donnie," one of the boatsmen called forward. "Just o'er a fathom."

Donovan knew they were close. The measurement meant that the bottom of the Channel was only eight or so feet beneath them. A few more pushes ahead, and the low fog suddenly began to part and a dull orange light began to fill the sky. Donovan was looking back at Johnay and the boatsman when the light changed. It hit the others' eyes first and reflected like moonlight catching a cat on the prowl. Johnay noticed first, took a step backwards, and almost stumbled off the boat. Carr had to prop him up.

"Dear God," Johnay's jaw quivered. In a moment, all the Rats were equally slack-jawed and wide-eyed. Then, it was Donovan's turn to look. What he saw took his breath away.

The waterfront of Rhodes Colony was a massive tangle of docks, sailing ships, and more modern metal vessels. Crowded warehouses and storage buildings rose up behind them, each covered with LED and neon signage, all flashing commercial announcements, advertisements, and colorful logos. A rainbow of color spread into the misty air. It was like nothing the Brothers and Sisters of the Sword had ever seen. Even in his small foray into the Empire, Donovan had seen a vastly different sight, a carefully pristine one, almost sparse and antiseptic, even in all its accompanying vastness. The Empire smacked of total order; the Colonies looked like organized chaos. They looked real and alive.

Donovan smiled as he checked his father's book and directed his boats to a lone long stretch of darkness to the right of the docks. "Forty-five degrees starboard," he pointed, his voice rising to the pitch of a commander, "that beach 'tis ours!"

Just across Thames Street, Mense took out a small digital spyglass and pulled it to his face.

"What is it?" The move put KZ on alert.

In his viewfinder, Mense could see Donovan and his five flat-boats heading for the shore. He zoomed in and saw closer. He saw the Empire Builder tattoo on Donovan's arm. He didn't know who they were, but it was certainly clear what they were. They were a tidy profit. Mense handed the binoculars to KZ with a smile. "Looks like there's more coin to be made tonight."

KZ took the spyglass and looked. Her face twisted through a range of scenarios. Finally, she lowered the glasses and just stared back at her lieutenant. "Sewer Rats?"

She quickly shot down his smile.

"Not our business." She pressed the spyglass back into his chest.

"Are you not a patriot, KZ?" he pushed her. "These are our Colonies, too."

This time, she let him put his hand on her shoulder. They had a history, one that despite her occasional flashes of empathy, KZ decided would not repeat.

"If we catch Sewer Rats tryin' to move on the Colonies," Mense plotted, "not only are we due for a pretty rock, but it'll make us bombproof with the Council and even, maybe, the Empire!"

KZ blinked. She knew it might be their ticket out. If nothing else, it would put them much higher on the pecking order than

Crank, which would come in handy were they both to run afoul of General Goynes's investigation. Mense was right. They might never get another chance like this.

Out in the shallowing Channel, a hush fell over the flatboats of the Brothers and Sisters of the Sword. Each teen was left to their own thoughts, hopes, and dreams. But just as they were able to wrap their individual brains around the possibilities of what may await them, they drew close enough to the beach to make out more.

Beyond the warehouses and storage depots, NewTown rose high into the hills behind. It was literally piled on top of itself, mostly consisting of newer versions of the Sewer buildings stacked and cut into the hill, on and on, rising hundreds of feet high. That wasn't the real sight, however. Carr, Gray, and the others unconsciously pushed their way forward as the vast and distantly glowing mountain range of Empire City rose far beyond. While many of the lights of the Colonies looked like flickering candles in the breeze, Empire City was like a sparkling mountain of crystal.

As the flatboats made for the beach, they silently slid close enough to see that many of the ships in the port bore a flag, a white field containing a golden anchor and a blue banner emblazoned with a single word.

Johnay read aloud what everybody could already see. "Hope."

Carr finally managed her first real smile. "Well, I'll be ground at t'stone." She came up to Donovan's side. "Almost to t'Empire itself."

Gray poked at Donovan's arm and directed him to one of the more modern vessels. Flying above those was the unmistakable blue and gold crown of the Empire.

Donovan smirked back and caught the eyes of Johnay, Crispus, and Gray. "Made it further than I thought already," he joked.

A few tense minutes later, the first of the flatboats landed softly, followed by the others. Nearly fifty teens clambered ashore through the filthy, rocky beach. All seemed quiet and secure. Off in the near distance, the streets of Rhodes hung in the mist. Donovan stopped his crew behind a sea wall and took out his father's book. As his brother and sister Rats took up positions behind him, he gathered Johnay, Crispus, Carr, and Gray to his side.

"We move this way." He pointed away from the Lawbroker station his father had drawn on the map. "We cross Thames there." Donovan traced the route on the paper. "Then, we split up and find places t'hide. With any fortune, t'four o' us will meet up at t'Red Fez three days hence."

The grim and determined faces nodded back as Donovan tried to give them all a reassuring smile. "Ready the smoke and mirrors." He arched a brow. "Got a feelin' we're gonna need it."

Carr, Johnay, Gray, and Crispus moved off to lead their own groups. Johnay's group was left by the boats, where they unloaded some gear and supplies. Donovan thought about his father's words:

Those who want to reap the blessings of freedom must, like men, undergo the fatigues of supporting it.

Across a field of debris, low seawalls, and fences, KZ and her gang waited. Up ahead, Donovan's group slowly made their way from the rocks and sand towards the first set of obstacles, piles of stone, and metal barricades.

KZ leaned over to Mense as she watched the maneuvers. "Not gonna be much to collect, I'm afraid," she gestured towards the metal obstacles. "They're headed right into the traps."

Donovan stopped by a low wall to survey the beachfront. It was lightly populated, just a few night workers strolling past, along with the occasional car or transport. Great shadows cut across the field from several directions. Plenty of places to hide. The other groups fanned out, boom sticks at the ready.

Donovan and his group moved up though the rocks and entered the field of jagged metal obstacles. They were half-buried in the sand and pitted with hungry rust. Nobody noticed the buried metal step plates hidden around them. Fifty feet to Donovan's right, Crispus was the first to make a misstep. The "traps" that KZ referred to were spring loaded steel spikes that, when triggered, flew up from the dirt in four directions, corroded barbs at the ends. The first trap flew up under Crispus's foot and knocked him sideways. He didn't fall, though; the fast-moving barb-covered arm caught him in the thigh and held him just long enough for the second arm to slam him straight in the chest. Blood and breath raced from his body in a macabre competition to hit the beach. Crispus barely made a sound; only the creak and grind of the killing device settling into final position spoke the final words on his behalf.

Before the others could even react, Rat Traps fired up all over the beach; blood, screams, and groans flew into the night as half of Donovan's Brothers and Sisters of the Sword were cut down. Many of them were lifted into the air by the hinged weapons, left to bleed and die like human scarecrows.

Back at the flatboats, Johnay saw everything slow down. As the others rushed past him to help, he backed up and fell into the cold water. He froze there, completely crippled by the sight. There, he watched as more bodies flew up like the dead popping out of graves. He softly whimpered and gulped at each and every one.

119

Halfway through the maze of beach, Donovan was grabbed and thrown down by a huge hand. It was Gray. Gray had pulled himself from a Rat Trap that had only winged him through the side.

"Now we know where they are. We can get 'round the rest," he directed ahead.

There was no time to dwell on the dead. Donovan signaled to Carr to lead her group around to the left. He grabbed Gray by the shoulder. "Can you lead?"

Gray nodded.

"Get back t'your group, We're pushin' through."

KZ and Mense watched the carnage from across Thames Street.

"We need to move now, before somebody calls in the Lawbrokers to take the coin." Mense waited for KZ's ok.

She was clearly still conflicted about it all, but after spying Mense and more of her group ready to fight, she nodded.

Mense smiled as he looked back to the others. "Payday, boys!"

KZ's group then moved across Thames Street, set up by the last of the seawalls, and opened fire.

Donovan, who had been unarmed, grabbed a boom stick from a fallen comrade and opened fire back—not at anything in particular, but at least to cover his own movements. Between shots, he crawled from obstacle to obstacle, stopping at a wet lump of debris that revealed itself as the body of one of his group. It took four more bullets for him.

Donovan dropped the boom stick as he recoiled from the lifeless lump. A shot from one of KZ's gang found his arm and he fell back and clutched at the small red fountain pulsing from under the sleeve of his long coat. All around him was death and suffering. Dead or dying teens lay fallen; others steadfastly returned fire, others stood, others fell, more died. The scene dulled into a blur as Donovan froze. He thought about dying. As he slumped, the thought led him to a passage in his father's book:

> The harder the conflict, the more glorious the triumph. What we obtain too cheap, we esteem too lightly; it is only dearness that gives everything its value. I love the man that can smile in trouble, that can gather strength from distress and grow.

Donovan leaned on the quote as he retrieved the boom stick, climbed to his feet and braced to lead a new charge forward. As he stood in the fusillade of projectiles, he smiled and glanced back to his Brothers and Sisters of the Sword. He screamed, "FREEDOM OR DEATH!" and took off around the suspended bodies, the dead and dying, charging forward not with reckless abandon but with purpose, determination, and history on his mind. With a thundering cheer, the others followed.

Deeper inside the deadly maze, Donovan called to his troops, "Brothers and Sisters of the Sword! POSITIONS! SMOKE AND MIRRORS ON MY SIGNAL!"

Across the way, KZ, Mense, and the rest of the Black-Flag Colonial gang stopped to watch the macabre sight.

Mense shot KZ a confused and wary look. "What's the damn fool think he's doin'?"

KZ took aim at Donovan's chest. "Trying to change his place in the world." She fired, but the shot only pierced the side of Donovan's billowing coat.

"Losing yer edge." Mense took an opportunity to flirt. KZ moved away from him just as the Rats struck back.

Behind Donovan, his remaining soldiers rushed forward and jammed makeshift reflectors into the ground. In front of those, they ignited hot-white incendiary magnesium flares suspended behind small polished-glass lenses. Rows of other Rats fired a barrage of the same small, bundled smoke bombs that Donovan had used to escape the Sewer guard in Perimeter Five. The sky quickly filled with smoke and beams of light, even as the ground below filled with blood and guts.

A teen in front of Carr took a steel ball to the head trying to set up one of the mirrors. Carr ducked behind the body and finished the job.

Behind the chaos, Johnay lay pinned in the first of the flatboats, bullets and projectiles slowly opening the bow of the boat beyond him, one small and deadly hole at a time. He shut his eyes preparing to die just as three other Rats came back to fetch and protect him. Two were put down by the Colonial gang's fire, their twitching bodies falling onto Johnay accompanied by a small waterfall of blood. Turned to stone by terror, only Johnay's voice seemed to obey his will. He cried out but left the bodies there to shield him.

From KZ's perspective, the beach became a confusing blur of smoke and blinking lights. Long shadows moved inside the growing blur. It looked like total panic.

"Poor bastards don't know what's hitting them," Mense observed.

Donovan's voice screamed out from the madness. "PRIME, LOAD AND FIRE! FRONT RANK! BAYONETS! FORWARD!"

"Neither do we," KZ huffed as she stood stiffly and faced her gang. She suddenly wondered if these Rats were far more dangerous than she'd bargained for. The answer came quickly as another battle cry erupted within the smoke and a spray of bullets came her way. Several of her gang took shots and KZ stumbled back at the sight of her own boys and girls screaming and bleeding. If she entertained any thoughts of withdrawal, they were gone. This fight was going to play out to a bloody end.

Donovan's Brothers and Sisters of the Sword let out a final blood-curdling battle cry as they began their final charge. "FREEDOM OR DEATH!"

"MORTARS NOW! GRAPESHOT!" a wide-eyed KZ screamed, as behind her the rear guard of her gang quickly set up two tripods containing central metal tubes. They loaded them with cloth and wire-bundled balls of shrapnel and fired them into the air.

The grapeshot hit the beach and its random splash of hot metal took down more of Donovan's crew, but they kept on coming.

Mense and KZ had no idea where their adversaries were in the smoke, and even less of an idea just when they'd arrive at the last seawall. "LIGHT THEM UP!" KZ screamed as her rear guard fired flares into the sky. It was a last resort. Now all would be revealed, and the battle would end in desperate and vicious hand-to-hand combat.

More grapeshot arrived on the battlefield. One stray shell landed in Johnay's flatboat. He heard the metal ping and watched frozen in shock as the smoking bundle lay there just out of his reach, a tiny fuse burning towards it for a final explosive moment. Johnay knew it was time to move but he could not reach it. He screamed out as he tried to struggle free of the dead bodies atop him. He knew he wasn't going to get free in time, but he persevered just the same. His fingers scraped off the grapeshot as he frantically struggled, but he was only able to push the deadly device another inch away. He reached again but missed as the small fuse vanished into the bundle. Then, with inhuman strength, he shirked the two bodies off and grabbed the projectile. It was out, harmless, a dud. Johnay threw it over the side anyway and collapsed back into the flatboat, where he sobbed and convulsed to breathlessness. His body motion set the flatboat adrift and it slowly began to float back into the Channel.

From inside the lingering smoke, KZ saw the worst possible scenario materializing. Donovan was leading about fifteen angry, screaming, and desperate Sewer Rats to the final seawall. Many of the sentry guards in Donovan's group were crack shots. As they got close, they quickly felled a half dozen of KZ's men before reloading and charging anew. Donovan and the rest of his troop had affixed jagged and filthy knives to the end of their boom sticks. This was not going to end well for anybody.

For the first time that night and in a long, long time, KZ took a step back. She turned right into Mense, who was clearly terrified of what was about to happen.

"THIS ISN'T WORTH THE COIN!" Mense shouted over the screams of the Rats, "WE HAVE TO PULL BACK!"

KZ knew that the die was cast. Stand fast or die. "I'M NOT RUNNING FROM GODDAMN SEWER RATS! MORE GRAPESHOT! WIPE THEM OUT! THEN MOVE IN FOR THE STRAGGLERS!" she commanded.

As Donovan and his group neared the wall, the beach erupted in mortar fire. Bodies flew every which way but the Rats kept coming. Carr's body took the brunt of a blast meant for Donovan, the small baubles of death cutting her side open like a butcher's knife. Donovan had no time to ponder; he took to the seawall and skewered one gang member before shooting another.

Out in the Channel, the sobbing Johnay realized his flatboat was moving. He peeked up over the edge and found himself a hundred yards offshore. Ahead of him on the beach, rockets lit the sky, and smoke trailed towards the bulk of NewTown. It looked like a war. He just watched and drifted further and further away.

8

BROADSIDE

HIGH ON THE HILL OVERLOOKING the NewTown docks, a familiar blue and gold crown flickered on the side of an imposing stone structure. Inside the local Constabulary post of Rhodes Colony, word of the ruckus on the beach came to the attention of the local Lawbrokers. Inside the medieval-themed control center, three concentric rings of glowing monitors sat manned by dozens of silhouetted figures. The images on the screens came via the hundreds of security cameras scattered around NewTown and Prudence Town beyond, along with readouts and GPS data from the equally scattered Lawbroker positions and patrols.

Leaning over one of the monitors was Lawbroker Lee Cruz, the scene of the beach attack spilling out onto Thames Street filling her eyes with dread. Was it a local gang fight? Was it an attack from another Colony? She tried to make sense of it all. Then as the smoke cleared, so did her thoughts. The combatants reaching the seawall weren't Colonials—they looked like Sewer Rats. If she turned for her superior's chair, she better have something good to bring to his attention.

In the center of this vast electronic semicircle of monitors and Lawbrokers, perched on a high throne-like chair sat Lord Thomas Hall Gage. In the flickering light, his face appeared a chiseled frieze of moods—mostly impatience, indifference, and resignation.

Looking him and his expressions over, Cruz thought better of it and returned to the monitor.

"I need to get closer," she commanded the analyst seated nearby.

"Buy some new cameras," he groused back.

Cruz was about to turn away and give up when she spotted the shape of Donovan Washington Rush on the screen. She pulled away from the image as every drop of blood in her body raced to the center of her chest. Cruz lifted her tablet computer to the terminal. "Send me that feed." She could barely utter the command. She was breathless.

The analyst obliged.

Cruz glanced up again at Gage, who was reading a tablet of his own. *Probably checking the lacrosse scores and his fight bets.* She shook her head. Still, she had her job to do. Tablet clutched to her side, Cruz paced over and climbed to Gage's elevated level. He noticed her there but didn't take his eyes from his screen.

"Watchman?" he said with a hint of annoyance.

Cruz lifted the tablet over his own. He frowned and darted two offended eyes her way.

"What are you bothering me with this for?" He dismissed it with a brush of his hand. "Local Colonial problem, not ours."

Cruz had done her homework tonight. "Reports from the Imperial Intelligence indicate that some Colonial customs security was bought by a Rhodes gang so they could close a smuggling deal…."

The grouping of "smuggling" and "Imperial Intelligence" captured Gage's attention, if only to bristle further. "What reports?"

"Some new investigation headed up by a…" Cruz pulled the tablet away to recheck the name.

Gage's eyes followed the image until it was out of sight. He was interested now.

"Looks like a Magistrate general by the name of John Goynes, Constable." Cruz eyed him back.

Gage extended his fingers and beckoned for the tablet now. He took what seemed a casual look, but clearly the wheels were turning in his head. "So, it's a black market street fight then? So what?" He tried to maintain an authoritative distance. "If it doesn't affect Imperial business or income, it's the taxman's problem, not ours."

Cruz swept her hand over a frozen image on the screen. It was the lifeless body of Crispus, hanging on the Rat Trap. There it was plain as day, the tattoo of an Empire Builder.

"Sewer Rat?" Gage muttered through a slackening jaw. "Impossible."

Cruz pulled up the image of Donovan next, his arms raised as he was about to bayonet a member of KZ's gang. There it was, the same tattoo.

Gage's eyes flashed as his mind raced with implications. If these kids were indeed Sewer Rats, this was the biggest breach of the Colonies in recent history. If he could bring it down, Gage could make quite the name for himself in the Empire. "Is that all?" he challenged her, hoping for more proof to cover him.

Cruz indeed had more. "Last week, there was that reported Rat break-in from Sector Five into the Keep."

"Report says the Rat was terminated." Gage flicked through the digital file and dismissed it.

Cruz pulled up the image from her own patrol craft the night she and Lawbroker Tarleton spotted Donovan Washington Rush, trapped like a deer in their searchlights. "I'm not so sure." She waited.

"Alright." Gage sighed. "Take a patrol. Look into it." He rubbed his brow. "Report back to no one but me, is that clear?" He barely waited for her nod. "And be discreet!"

Cruz hid her smile as she turned. She didn't get far, and her smile didn't last long.

Standing in the shadows at the back of the room, watching the conversation unfold, was Lawbroker Silas Tarleton. Cruz blinked at the sight. *Ever the tactician,* she thought. *Always waiting for the right moment to attack.* As if on cue, Tarleton sashayed over like an indifferent king walking through his court.

"Not tonight, Watchman Cruz." Tarleton coolly brushed past her. "It's my job to give the lads a clap on the shoulder, not yours."

Without so much as a blink, Cruz stared into Tarleton's eyes. It took him a second to find the hatred there. He simply smiled, then cocked his head to Gage expectantly.

Gage nodded. "Take charge, lieutenant."

Donovan and the last twelve of his crew were over the seawall, and a furious hand-to-hand battle ensued. The deadly melee spilled onto the nearby docks and across Thames Street. A crowd of late-night dockworkers and warehouse loaders approached but stayed a safe distance. They thought it a gang fight and nobody wanted any part of that. In the chaos, bodies were skewered by makeshift bayonets, bullets, and steel balls that ripped into flesh at close range. Screams of fury and death filled the air.

KZ knew her gang was about to be overrun. So did Mense. He grabbed her arm. "We have to go, now!"

She stopped him and shoved him back, a plan burned behind her eyes. "Pull back to Warehouse 17." She was coldly determined. "Set up a choke!"

Mense nodded and grabbed three others and took off, just as Donovan fought his way into the center of the chaos and burst through to Thames Street. It looked like KZ's Rhodes gang was pulling back.

"This way!" he directed them, as KZ's badly depleted gang made room. Donovan and seven survivors were off into a dark alley across Thames Street. As they passed under a rusted old sign for Warehouse 17, shots rang out. POP! POP! POP! KZ had set up her impromptu firing squad in a choke point at the end of the alley. One of Donovan's crew got off a return shot; the others were dead before they could even aim.

Another shot found Donovan in his already winged left shoulder. This shot was true. It ripped into deep tissue and muscle and grazed the bone before taking off a chunk of Donovan's shoulder blade. The pain was like being immersed in fire. It was paralyzing. It turned his vision red and cloudy and plunged his mind into a chaos of instinct and fear. As the leader of the Sons and Daughters of the Sword slumped to one knee, the dirty walls and distant rooftops of the Colonies spun into a dizzying haze.

Donovan hung there, his head bowed, as saliva dripped from his slack open mouth. After a beat, KZ emerged from the shadows and slowly walked over to circle him. She paced around and around to size him up and then kicked his wounded shoulder. Donovan cried out as the pain brought back his focus. He hit the cobblestones and looked up, locking eyes with his female opponent.

"You cost me a lot of men tonight, Rat." KZ kicked him in the back, driving his face into the uneven road. "Reward for killing you won't even begin to set this right."

Donovan saw through the blood and pain as KZ walked around him again. *If I die,* his mind cleared, *I die a free man.*

Instead of finishing him, KZ crouched down near his face and waited for his eyes to focus on her. She then pulled out a long stylized blade and brought it to Donovan's neck. "Freedom's what you came here for…well, here it comes…."

As KZ drew the blade back, Donovan reached under his coat and retrieved a magnesium flare like the ones used for the smoke and mirrors tactic. With a quick motion, he struck the small metal chunk on the stone and it lit to a thousand degrees. Before KZ could move, it was in her thigh and, as the searing pain shot through her, KZ raked the knife across Donovan's throat, but the sensory overload had compromised her perception and all she managed was a long scrape and slight cut. She instantly fell back screaming as the blade left her grip and clanged away.

Mense and KZ's snipers readied to fire again, but Donovan tossed the white-hot flare at them and, in the bright flash of confusion, scurried away. Mense quickly stopped the group from firing.

"NO! You'll hit KZ!"

"THERE!" One of the snipers thought he saw Donovan headed out from the choke point. POP! POP! POP! The others opened fire at the shadows. Nothing.

"STOP!" KZ shrieked as she jumped up. "He's mine!" She quickly scrambled for her knife and was off.

Donovan bolted back onto Thames Street, pushed through a small crowd, and turned up another dark alley parallel to the next dockside warehouse. As the knife-wielding KZ rushed out behind, the uneasy crowd was all too happy to point out the Rat's route.

Down the next alley, Donovan found another dead end, but there were barrels and crates piled up against the warehouse—and maybe a way to reach the roof. Despite the pain of his shoulder, long since drowned in a torrent of fear and adrenaline, Donovan lifted himself up towards the roof, but it was no good. To the side, a decent jump away was a drainpipe.

KZ ran up under the scene, and when Donovan saw her, he made the desperate leap. The drainpipe screamed and partially ripped from the building. Donovan fell instantly, but the drainpipe caught his waistcoat. Seeing this, KZ leapt into the crates and climbed. But before she could get to him, Donovan got his arms free and grabbed the broken drain and pulled himself up. KZ thought of throwing the knife until she spied in the darkness an access ladder to the roof on the opposite side of the crates.

Stunned, exhausted, and slowly bleeding out, Donovan pulled himself to the roof and rolled over. Gasping for breath and expecting to die, he looked for a shred of hope in the tatters of night.

Instead, he got a knife in his back courtesy of KZ.

As he instinctively rolled to the side to defend his life, Donovan broke the blade in half. His reaction to the crippling pain was to roll again. This time, the move carried both Donovan and KZ off the other corner of the roof, down a four-foot drop, and through the top of a rusted shed on the adjacent roof.

The old corrugated tin cut into both KZ and Donovan like a giant steel claw as they passed through it. They landed, winded and bleeding, on a workbench, splintering it into several sharp pieces, many of which found more skin and muscle to puncture. Donovan had more to lose, and a final burst of survival adrenaline brought him to his senses first. Before KZ could react, he grabbed a shard of corrugated metal and plunged it into her side. KZ fell back, wide-eyed and frightened. Dying from anything other than old age was never on her list. Dying to be free was Donovan's entire mission.

In KZ's moment of fear, Donovan paused on her face, beautiful, blood-stained, and utterly vulnerable. In the slivers of light entering the shed, she looked like a painting from an old book, a frozen canvas of wonder and fleeting life. KZ seized the moment back and used Donovan's pause to her advantage. She gracefully rolled up from her knees and, with a rage-filed grunt, kicked him through the far wall of the shed and out onto the adjacent roof. She then grabbed one of the sawed-off table legs like a dagger and leaped out after him.

Outside again, KZ found Donovan back on his feet and keeping his distance.

"I'll make a deal with you." KZ spit out a clump of her own blood. "Let me take you in, and I'll let you live."

Donovan tensed as she tried to maneuver closer. He'd lost a lot of blood; his vision was slowly fading to gray and red. His entire body felt and moved like it was under ten feet of water.

"If you let me go," he rasped, "I'll have my army spare ya."

She let her guard down to lure him in. "An army of the dead?" She smirked. "Deal's off!" KZ barely let the words end as she leapt into the air, the wooden dagger aimed straight at Donovan's heart.

He stopped the blow, the dagger going just past his neck, but KZ's momentum carried them both to the ground, where they struggled over the wooden weapon as they rolled again into the warehouse wall. Slowly, Donovan's strength ebbed and the dagger drew closer and closer to his neck. Slowly, all of his strength melted and his body began to go limp. KZ stopped for a moment. She looked down at her helpless foe. She suddenly didn't want to kill him like this. It seemed incongruous to her world view of balance and justified equilibrium. The few seconds of indecision was all it took for the blood loss to catch up to her, too. She suddenly spasmed as her vision clouded and a pain shot through her temples and down to her feet. She suddenly wobbled and shuddered as the dagger fell out of her hand. "Blast it all," KZ muttered as she tried to reach again for the weapon.

Donovan blinked up at her. To him, she faded into an amorphous shape, a gray ghost hovering in the air. The ghost moved to the side as KZ stumbled again. There, she materialized again and used the last of her strength to regain the dagger. Using two hands, she raised it over her head.

Donovan squinted now as a bright white light formed behind her. *The doorway to death,* he thought. For a moment, all Donovan could see was her shadow as it seemed to look back over its shoulder. It looked to Donovan as if death had come for them both.

It was the bluish searchlight of a manta-shaped Lawbroker craft—Lawbroker Tarleton and Watchman Cruz's Lawbroker craft. Illuminated by the flickering lights of the cockpit, Tarleton glanced casually at Cruz as he let the nets fly. These two were worth more alive. Cruz knew that, much like the Empire she served, Tarleton sought both the glory and the coin.

Donovan awoke restrained to a bed, the room around him dark and murky. As his eyes struggled to find a reference point, only shapes and shadows materialized, and all he could make out in the fog was a couple of blinking monitoring machines and a shadowed lump across the way. When he tried to move his arms and legs, they didn't comply.

Donovan's first thought was that he was paralyzed, but strangely, he could feel the bed under him. It was a complete relief to find that he was merely restrained. The realization buoyed him, bringing more light to his eyes. There was still hope. He could see that it was a hospital room now. There was a bed across from him. The air tasted sweet. He then felt a slight pressure against his face. He was wearing an oxygen mask. As Donovan struggled to lift his head, his strength gave out again and everything went black.

Outside in the unclean halls of the Rhodes Colonial Hospital, Watchman Cruz, now in plain clothes, waited at a viewing window, assessing her next moves. Inside the room were both Donovan and KZ, two prizes in the Colonial game of Lawbroker power and glory. Cruz thought about how they now both belonged to Tarleton. That was the pecking order…for now. Maybe she could still find some opportunity here. Both she and her foil in the Constabulary knew Donovan's identity, but right here, right now, with Tarleton busy taking credit for the arrest, she had a slim opportunity to know more, so she slid within earshot of the two guards from the Rhodes Colonial Police who were standing watch in the hall behind her.

"Huaxian girl's pretty well up with some on the Council…" one commented.

"She's a looker." The other guard was focused on more primal matters.

"Killed a lotta Rats tonight, too…. Got some pretty coin coming to her for her trouble," the first guard continued.

Cruz turned to the two men. "What about the other one?" She gestured. "The boy?"

The second guard shrugged. "Not a shred of identification on him…just some journal book and some kinda bauble he knucked from the Empire."

"Bauble?" Cruz eyed them as the first guard shot a look to his partner to shut up.

"Who wants to know?" The first guard suddenly bristled.

Cruz flashed her Constabulary badge. It didn't impress the guard.

"I outrank a Watchman around here." He grinned.

"Didn't you see his Builder mark?" Cruz smirked.

The two exchanged a glance.

"Donovan Washington Rush. Dogue Run, Fairfax Flats," she offered them a bit of information in bargain. They were stunned she already knew so much. It made them nervous. "Now, about that bauble?" Her eyes narrowed.

"Some bit of Empire jewel," the first guard grumbled. "If' he croaks, I'm takin' it." He was challenging her for the spoils. "I may just pilfer it anyway."

"Any other effects beside the book you mentioned?" Cruz didn't even blink.

"The girl only had some electronics, the usual personal stuff."

"Where are they?"

"Left 'em in the drawer beside them." The guards eyed her warily now.

Cruz nodded and turned for the door. The first guard stepped in to block her path. "No entry under orders of the Council and Lieutenant Tarleton," his tone grew dismissive and superior, "watchman."

Cruz produced her tablet and woke it up. She brought her electronic pen to the surface. "What are your names?" She eyed them coldly.

It didn't work. The guards just looked bored.

"You two cow-coats know who Constable Gage is?"

They two men looked at each other. Everybody in Rhodes Colony knew.

"Care to meet him?" she pressed, a slight smile curling onto her lips.

The guard blinked and moved aside. "Two minutes."

Cruz slid past. "I just need a few seconds to process the evidence."

The first guard stared down his partner and followed her in. Cruz went straight for the drawer next to Donovan and opened it. The book was still wet with blood, and the unnerving Empire pin was covered with grease and dirt. The pin caught Cruz off guard. She knew what it was.

"Problem?" The first guard hovered near her shoulder.

She blocked his view as she scanned the drawer with her tablet, recording the contents and filing the details. "Did you look in here?" She put on her best authoritative voice.

The tone set the guard on edge. "No, ma'am; duty nurse saw it, though."

Cruz rubbed the dirt from the pin and saw the logo. On the side of the small device was a hidden clasp. She flicked it, and the pin opened to a tiny forest of electronics. She passed the tablet over it and hid from the guard that she had just gotten a lock on the signal—the same lock that Dr. Franklin had. Then, as she closed the drawer on the guard, she used a glimpse at the tablet to distract him from her other hand, which skillfully slipped the book into her coat. She then just shut the drawer and paced across the room towards KZ. The guard followed.

"Colonial gang member, you say?" she inquired offhandedly.

"Leader, but she got friends on the Council. We're supposed to watch her close, but I'd wager she'll be back on t'streets soon."

Cruz nodded as she looked over KZ, then turned for the door. "Thank you," she made nice with the guard. "They're all yours."

As she neared the threshold to the hall, Cruz stopped and looked back. "Sleep well, little Sewer Rat," she whispered. "My guess is you'll be avoiding the hangman's noose too. Seems you've got friends in high places." Cruz then took one last glance out the room window and towards the gigantic and distant mountain range that was Empire City. For a moment, she thought about living there. Then, she walked into the hall.

Behind her, KZ cracked open her eyes to watch. She had been listening the entire time.

Lawbroker Lieutenant Tarleton was waiting in the hall. The Colonial Guard—or cow-coats, as they were called—were even more uneasy now that a decorated and higher-ranking Lawbroker was here.

Tarleton ignored them and pushed right to Cruz. His tone and words were more accusation than question. "Find anything?"

Cruz shook her head and gestured to the guards as if they couldn't be trusted. She led Tarleton by the eyes further down the hall where she just shook her head again.

"You wouldn't be holding out on me again like you did with that Rat's ID would you now, watchman?"

Cruz knew Tarleton was, as usual, in no mood for any way but his own. She had something and she knew he could see it in her eyes. She saw into his as well. For a moment, he seemed worried if she had found enough to push her career past his own. Tarleton blinked and suddenly smiled. "Maybe we can do business, Cruz." He reached out his hand and let his fingertip slip across her chin.

Cruz pulled away, a death stare in her eyes. "I'd rather be sent to rot in the Sewers."

"And fed to the Rats?" Tarleton chuckled before his expression went cold again. "Perhaps I can arrange that."

"They're not expected to make it, lieutenant." She turned partly away from him. "You'd just be wasting what tiny slivers of character and honor you have left on me." Her heart racing from her theft and play, Cruz strained to stay composed as she walked away.

High in his Magistrate Tower office, Dr. Richard Franklin closely watched his tablet map and the tiny blip that was Donovan Washington Rush as it hovered inside the boundaries of Rhodes Colonial Hospital. Franklin had spent the last three hours watching the electronic signal exit the coastal waters of the Channel and into Rhodes. His heart pounded as the movement stalled on the beach and then, once back in motion, went as far as the warehouse complex across Thames Street. When it froze there, Franklin froze, too. He suspected the worst, but the blip suddenly jumped back to life and made a high-speed move from NewTown twenty miles north to Rhodes Hospital in Prudence Town. It only meant one thing: a violent apprehension by the Constabulary followed by a medivac for treatment.

Franklin suddenly wondered about the Magistrate pin he'd given to Donovan. It would be hard to trace to him directly, but it would present a great and dangerous mystery just the same. Franklin's friend General Goynes was right to suspect him. Franklin was well known in the Magistrate's circle as an evolutionary force and only partly appreciated for it. Even as an absolute ruler, His Magistrate William Frederick was not without a sense of social justice, but that sense was far removed from the people by time, monarchist history, and the oft-clueless arrogance that arises from the combination. William Frederick the Third kept Franklin around as much to excuse his power as to temper it. Still, the post of such a high advisor offered Franklin the kind of protection and immunity that the Colonials referred to as being *bombproof*.

Others in the Imperial power structure weren't so mindful of striking such balance. Most, including Goynes, saw Franklin's ideas as dangerous to absolute authority. Franklin saw their view for what it was: absolute power, corrupted absolutely. The entire scenario tonight, Franklin's prodding of Donovan to action, had already gone far further than even he imagined. His original intent was just to give the son back some of what was taken from the father, a way to make up for the boy's family being locked away by the Empire to a sentence of living death. Now, it was all critically close to the point of no return, and Franklin was left to ponder that this could cost him his life in the worst case, but might also achieve the impossible, too—a transformation of his Empire.

He was hiding more complex and darker concerns as well. Franklin was a member of the Hellfire Society, a clandestine ancient order of spies for the Crown. It was part of Franklin's brilliant chess game: move through the murky circles of the Empire's intelligence underground, have a level of information even beyond His Magistrate, and, from this position, make the most opportune moves available. Goynes was right; he and Franklin were far more similar than the good doctor would have admitted, but Franklin was playing both sides of the board, and, for now, hadn't quite decided which was the lesser of two evils.

Rather than take too hasty a set of actions, Franklin decided to stall and push things further. He felt at this early stage that he could likely find a way to further hide his moves. His own curiosity was the real trap. He almost had to see what might happen next and was willing to take a bigger risk to do so. What he didn't realize was that he was indeed in too deep already. General Goynes was even more suspicious of him than he knew; not for this, but as an opponent on the field of political battle. For now, Franklin was temporarily blinded by Donovan, and the tiny seed he'd planted in the boy had been captured and coalesced, in a sense, in the Empire pin he carried.

Franklin used his access and Imperial tablet to check on the local Lawbroker chatter and intelligence news from Rhodes Colony. Among the links, he found the reports of the Black-Flag gang-related incident on NewTown Beach. Scanning down the hyperlinks, Franklin also found the report of gang members transported to Rhodes Colonial Hospital in Prudence Town.

A message flashed across his screen, ROXANNE, with a stylized avatar of a tiara and a sword. An encrypted message blinked below. Franklin gently stroked a finger across her name like a fond caress. After a soft and warm smile, he opened the message.

Arranged something fun for you. An evening of libation and information. Meet me at the Society later?

Wheels spinning ever faster, Dr. Franklin pondered and sat back. In a moment he quickly swiped away the message and reports, and opened the communications portal to request a secure Imperial channel.

"Scramble a secure channel to Rhodes Colony for me," he spoke into the device.

"Your P.I. Monitor is off, sir. Please identify yourself." A grim security officer's face popped up on the screen. Clearly, he was hitting several keys on his end trying to see who was calling.

"Priority level one," Franklin pushed.

"You must be measured, sir." The officer blinked, not really expecting Franklin had that level of clearance.

"Brother Cookham. Number Seventy-Two."

"Straight away." The officer was unnerved. The number identified Franklin as part of the I.I.S., the feared Imperial Intelligence Service.

"I'd like a word with the administrator of Rhodes Colonial Hospital," Franklin directed.

"Secure channel, right away, sir."

Franklin waited for the call to connect. In a few moments, the chiseled visage of the hospital administrator popped up. He seemed a gentle fellow, long, silver hair pulled into a ponytail and bushy gray beard.

"How may I serve His Magistrate this morning?" He forced a smile. Getting a call from the Empire was seldom good news.

"You have two new patients this evening?"

"We have over two dozen new arrivals."

"Two from NewTown, brought in by Lawbroker transport?"

"Yes." The remnants of the administrator's smile faded. "Some kind of gang incident."

"I see." Franklin massaged his broad chin. "Any Empire Builders among them?"

The administrator became confused and worried. "Why, as a matter of fact, yes."

"Under Constabulary guard, I take it?"

"That is correct." The administrator peered deep into his own tablet trying to read Franklin's face.

"Very well." Franklin's demeanor turned directive. "I'd like you to place a call to Governor Cooke and request that Colonial Council sentries be sent to relieve the Constabulary men on duty. See that the boy is not harmed."

The administrator didn't understand. Something was going on, as these two teens were suddenly important to the Empire.

"But you can…" he stammered.

142

"It would serve His Magistrate best, and you as well," Franklin said pointedly, "were the request to come from you and matters, therefore, remained at the Council level."

Before the administrator could even nod, Franklin cut the call.

Five miles to the west of the Magistrate Tower, the Imperial Ministry of Defense rose almost as high into the brightening morning sky. Inside his office, a sleeping General Goynes was slumped over his desk, reports strewn about. Three flatscreen monitors on the wall beyond him were full of information that was now hidden behind the Imperial screensaver of the blue and gold crown. His career aspirations in the balance, Goynes had immersed himself in his plan to catch the Huaxian smuggling operation in the Colonies. He had immersed himself to sleep. A young corporal entered to nudge him awake.

"What the hell do you want?" The cranky and half-asleep general kept his eyes closed as the young soldier placed a tablet report under his nose.

"Communications from the Magistrate Tower to Rhodes Colony, sir."

Goynes stirred slightly.

"Scrambled on the I.I.S. channel."

Goynes opened his eyes and lifted his head. "Imperial Intelligence?" He thought a beat. "Not our concern, corporal."

"The call went through just minutes after a Black-Flag dock fight in Rhodes Colony..." the young soldier continued.

Goynes straightened up and grabbed the tablet. "Who sent this?"

"We don't have access to that information." The corporal blinked. "But our sources on the investigation in the docks inform that a short while before, a secret exchange took place at the customs house." The lad eyed Goynes. "Two survivors of the battle were taken by Lawbrokers to Rhodes Hospital."

Goynes's eyes began to blaze. "I want to question them." He stood and grabbed his coat. "Have a shuttle ready to take me to Rhodes."

"Rhodes Colonial Governor Cooke has taken charge of the prisoners, sir." The corporal let the suspicion wash over his own face now. "Seems he wanted some of the glory, too. We'd need a Magistrate override to intervene."

"The governor of Rhodes has no business interfering with an Imperial investigation unless…" Goynes stopped the thought as he shoved his arms into his military coat.

"Sir?"

"Never mind, corporal." Goynes suddenly pulled his arms back out of the jacket. "Not a word of this, do you understand me?"

The corporal just stared at him.

Goynes smiled. "We don't want the game we hunt to know we're here. This sordid mess may go all the way to the Magistrate's inner council." He paced into shadow. "Why shoot one or two quail when you can shoot them all?"

The small flatboat creaked and moaned as it slowly filled with water and limped back towards the massive filtration gate outside Fairfax Flats. Johnay, blood all over his face and clothing, stood at the stern, quant pole in hand, the lifeless bodies of friends splayed across the floor of the craft before him. Arms aching and the last of his strength fading away, he staggered back and dropped the pole onto the boat and sat. The boat pushed ahead on its own and gently clanked off the front edge of the looming gate. Tears long-dried into a patina of hopelessness and desperation, Johnay just stared up at the gate. Slowly, rage pulled him back to his feet and he picked up the quant pole like a bat and swung it as hard as he could.

CLANG! CLANG! CLANG! The metal gate responded with an ominous and indifferent sound that was somewhere between a church bell and the impenetrable barrier it was. There was nothing but echoes. They washed across Johnay and out into the Channel before returning to taunt him. He swung four more times. Nothing.

"HEY! SOMEBODY! SOMEBODY! LET ME IN! LET ME INNNNNNNNN!" Johnay fell back onto the stern again and began to cry. He was alone amongst corpses. He was half dead.

"Somebody…please…" His voice retreated inwards, forcing a renewed flood of tears. The echoes of his despair seemed softer suddenly. It almost seemed to Johnay that there were other voices coming back; maybe more of his fallen shipmates had followed him. Slowly, he stopped sobbing and braced himself, stood back up on the boat, and grabbed at the steering pole. Just as he screwed up the courage to push back out to sea, his moves were interrupted by a terrible metal squeal. A rush of foul air flew out from the cracks as the massive filtration gate began to grind open.

The Sewers had opened to take him back.

Through the opening gate, Johnay saw nothing but darkness and despair. The low-hanging fog and familiar stench brought him home in his mind. As he nudged the flatboat into the canal, Johnay wondered if the Sewer Guards were waiting to catch him for the coin. Part of him no longer cared if he'd get home or be mustered out. As his eyes adjusted to the darkness, he scanned the catwalks above to see if he was being watched. He was.

"Welcome home," Captain White called out. He was still the leader of the Sewer Guard. It was unclear if it was a taunt or in earnest. The Sewer guard and his small troop looked down on Johnay and his boat, half flooded with water and half full with blood and entrails. "Looks as if y'had enough troubles fo' one night," one of the guards called down. "Let 'im pass!" White added.

Johnay fell back again onto the raised stern of the boat and slid down to the deck as the massive filtration gate boomed closed behind him. He then shut his eyes equally as hard, just as final.

Three sentries from the Governor's detachment strutted the halls of Rhodes Hospital towards Donovan and KZ's intensive care suite. The two Colonial guards bristled at their approach, but they had a digital order from the governor himself to stand down. "You Mules can leave," the lead Council guard sneered.

The first of the Colonial guards was the pudgier of the two. He knew what was going on and wanted to protest if for no other reason than to stoke his ego, but instead, his round face twisted into the same kind of expression a soiled baby makes when just about to cry. Then, he made a futile attempt at petty defiance and called his local dispatch to make sure the orders were legitimate.

As the shift change took place down the hall, KZ noticed that there were no more guards stationed outside the viewing port to the ICU. She turned her eyes towards Donovan. In her mind, the boy was responsible not just for her wounds, but for the decimation of her primary gang, the loss of a lot of rock, and a huge blot on her local reputation and influence. She wanted him dead, and this seemed her best chance.

Grimacing and grunting through the pain of her wounds, KZ dragged her battered and punctured body up from her bed. Two IV lines popped out of her as she moved, but she hardly noticed the pain—or the trail of blood droplets running down her gown. One shuffling foot at a time, KZ dragged herself towards the unconscious and helpless Donovan, and, as she stumbled, she looked for something to kill him with, a tube for strangling, maybe, or some kind of blade to cut his throat. She closed to within a few feet and saw that all of her planning was unnecessary. Donovan was not only hooked up to an oxygen supply, he was also hooked up to several other lines and machines that were keeping him stable and alive. That became KZ's primary goal: to pull the plug.

Checking the viewing window again, KZ could see the shapes of the four guards deep in conversation just down the hall. She turned back to her intended victim but stumbled again as her legs gave out. She was in no condition for standing, let alone murder, so she crawled backwards to one of her IV stands and locked the wheels. Painfully, she pulled herself back to her feet, kicked the wheel lock free, and moved in, using the stand for support. The oxygen supply and life-support machines were indeed hooked into an outlet on the wall beside Donovan's bed, but it was a long way to go. There was a pair of crutches leaning on a chair by the door, so KZ rode the IV stand as far as the chair and then switched to the crutches.

As soon as she got within reach of Donovan, she steadied herself as best she could and took a swipe at the oxygen line. It flew off Donovan's face, twisting his head to the side. She paused to watch, but he didn't awaken. Instead, his breath became labored and short. KZ smiled like a cobra might as its venom took hold until an alarm went off on one of the monitoring machines. KZ instantly lurched back and stumbled. She dropped the crutch and fell to one knee. The alarm was not that loud, but it obviously registered at the nearby nurse's station. With time running out, KZ used the other crutch to pull out the plug on the life support.

Donovan's body instantly convulsed and his spine arched into a horrible death twitch. KZ scrambled back to her bed and fell into it just as far louder alarms went off. Donovan was flatlining, moments from death.

Eyes wide, KZ lay back to watch the boy die. Before the nurses and guards responded, something in Donovan did. KZ watched in shock and wonder as a single tear silently ran down from his eye, then…nothing. Just as the nurses and guards burst in, Donovan suddenly shuddered and gasped awake, his eyes opening wide. He looked around the room, then stared directly at KZ like he knew what she'd just done. He was alive on his own, as if he was unwilling to accept death.

As the stunned nurses tried to figure out what happened, KZ recoiled from the sight. It terrified her. It seemed like divine intervention, like Donovan was meant for more. All KZ could do was slump back down and mutter in her childhood Huaxian dialect, "Feinikesei…Feinikesei…."

Donovan Washington Rush had just risen from the dead. A phoenix from the ashes.

9

A TURN OF THE COIN

WITH A CLEARLY IRRITATED Lawbroker Tarleton at his side, Constable Gage paced over to Watchman Cruz at her computer station. Once there, he motioned as Tarleton handed her a tablet full of orders.

"What's this?" She looked up.

"Public execution order." Tarleton looked excited by the very turn of the phrase.

"I don't understand." Cruz began to read.

"My informants have identified five filtration gate guards of the Fairfax Militia as those directly responsible for the breach."

"The breach?" Cruz noted the emphasis on "The," meaning there was more to it.

"Several hours ago, five boatloads of runaways got into the Channel," Tarleton explained.

Cruz blinked. She knew Tarleton had informants but not necessarily in the very Sewers. He was even more dangerous than he let on.

"That little skirmish at the docks this evening?" Tarleton shot her a raised eyebrow for effect.

"Half the victims were Sewer Rats," Constable Gage finished the sentence.

Cruz already knew, of course, but she'd hoped it would have taken more time for them to fit the pieces together; yet there were Gage and Tarleton, seemingly a step ahead of her.

"It's the largest Sewer escape in twenty years." Gage's eyes blazed as he slapped the order into Cruz's shoulder and turned away. "Get moving," he added with a growl. "Can't let the punishment linger, it'll look bad on the Empire."

Tarleton then added his own glare, one that let on that perhaps Cruz still had some leverage after all. He was reacting as if her bringing up the incident in Rhodes had thrust any misstep into his lap, too. Still, she knew that what really upset Tarleton wasn't the assignment, or Cruz bringing the entire incident to Gage's attention. It was that now Gage had leapfrogged Tarleton to the credit and money, so as unpleasant as an execution was, Cruz took a moment of satisfaction at Tarleton's expense. The moment didn't last.

Tarleton lingered to stare her down. "Take the old man with you." He smiled.

"Monty?" Cruz was confused.

"Sure. He could use a little excitement before his retirement."

"You're not leading this?" Cruz smelled an instant setup. Maybe Tarleton still had the upper hand after all.

"I want you to get full credit, Cruz." Tarleton snarled a fanged smile before sliding away.

It didn't feel right and Cruz knew why. It'd been years since the Constabulary or the Empire had held a public execution in the Sewers. If there were ramifications either locally or up in the

Empire, Cruz would be positioned as the sacrificial lamb, and Tarleton, it now seemed, was lumping Monty in with the same fate. Suddenly, Cruz felt like little more than a loose end.

Back in Dogue Run and Fairfax Flats, another form of execution was in the offing as Johnay, soaked with blood and brackish water, staggered into the meeting room at the Dogue Run home. As soon as he entered, Johnay relaxed to the point of safety, and that point is where his strength ebbed. He stumbled a few steps and slid against the wall where the "Freedom or Death" slogan was painted. Knox and Payne were before him, backs turned, looking over the map on the table, plotting their next moves into the Colonies.

"Nothing from my contacts in t'Sewer Guard." Knox's shoulders heaved through an exhausted sigh.

"'Tis this good or bad news?" Payne raked his hands through his long hair.

Knox could only shrug as he stared down at the map as if hoping to divine something new from its crudely painted shapes and symbols. With a deepening stare, he ran his palms and fingertips over the images until he got to the rough map of Rhodes that had been hastily added from Dr. Rush's book.

"'Cording to Donnie's father," Knox tapped his index finger on Rhodes, "there'll be those sympathetic t'our cause at this Red Fez." He took another breath. "Surely one of us'll make it."

"Not a soul made it," Johnay's voice rasped from the shadows.

Knox and Payne instantly slumped at the sight of Johnay, whose weary lean had smudged a streak of brown semi-dried blood across the word "Freedom" on the wall's slogan. It took a moment for Payne and Knox to gather their senses.

"Who did this?" Payne finally uttered.

Johnay was silent, locked between pain, rage, and defeat.

"Lawbrokers??" Knox pressed.

"Goddamn Rhodes gang," Johnay finally spit it out. "Fo' t'bloody coin."

"Donnie?" Payne gulped and uttered the fearful question.

Johnay just looked down at the floor as a single tear dropped from his eye. He just shook his head as the others tensed.

The room halted for several seconds more. Only the flickering sizzle of candles could be heard.

"The cause goes on," was all Knox could think of as he braced and propped his shoulders.

"Wot cause?!?" Johnay huffed as he approached the table, dropped his hands onto the map and hung his head. "Do y'honestly think t'Sewer Guard will e'er let us pass 'gain? We're all marked for t'Boxman now! 'Tis over!"

Payne grabbed Johnay's arm. "Brace up, man. Empire's strength comes from just this kind of fear…fear of resistance… loss of hope."

Johnay pulled away from Payne and slumped into a chair. He shook his head in utter despair. "It's done, Payne. T'Magistrate and Colonial Lawbrokers are gonna punish us fo' this. All we've done is set t'cause back a generation! Two generations. Three even!"

"I'll lead t'next o' t'boats then." Payne's voice grew stronger. "'Tis not just a struggle o' gettin' to t'Colonies, or for a few acres of ground. 'Tis cause o' t'whole Six Lands." Payne climbed to his feet and paced around the table. "'N' whether we defeat our enemy in one battle, af'er a thousand or by a degree, t'consequences will be the same."

Knox and Johnay locked eyes as Payne spoke. Finally, Johnay slowly nodded. There was nothing left to lose. The three teens then sat silent for a few beats until a low rumble began to fill the room, unsettling candles and shaking plaster and dust from the walls. Knox and Johnay jumped up as one of the sentries pulled open the balcony window and looked in. His face was locked in a stunned expression.

"'Tis an entire Lawbroker convoy!" he stammered. "T'big guns!"

Johnay, Knox, and Payne quickly climbed out to the top-floor balcony to watch. Ahead in the darkness, three massive Constabulary Battle Cruisers floated into Dogue Run, searchlights beaming from their undersides. On the back and sides of each, the lit crown logo of the Empire shone.

The battleships were covered near the top with viewing windows and turret bubbles. Rats all about King Street gathered into stunned groups, then scattered for fear of assembly reprisals, until a booming voice from the first of the cruisers commanded them to hold their ground. As the voice pierced the musty air and darkness, every single Empire proclamation screen in the Sewers lit up in deadly choreography. On every screen, the face of Watchman Lee Cruz stared unblinking in full combat attire.

"ATTENTION! ATTENTION, CITIZENS OF FAIRFAX! BY DECREE OF HIS MAGISTRATE WILLIAM FREDERICK THE THIRD, ASSEMBLY RULES ARE TEMPORARILY RESCINDED! THOSE IN THE STREETS BELOW ARE DIRECTED TO HOLD POSITION! REPEAT! STAY WHERE YOU ARE! YOU WILL NOT BE PUNISHED!"

The boys exchanged looks as the first of the transports slowed to a stop about fifty yards from the Dogue Run home. The other two fanned out behind and moved away into the distance. It was a defensive battle maneuver.

"Wot t'hell?" Johnay grabbed the balcony rail and squinted towards the first of the massive ships. On the rail, he could make out Lawbroker battle troops moving about.

"They've come f'us." Payne braced. "Not without a fight." He turned to the group home sentries. There was no place to run. The teens were trapped like the Rats they were.

"NO! LOOK!" Knox pointed as five manacled teens were shoved up on a higher portion of the deck among the group of moving shapes. Five more waited behind them.

Payne's eyes widened as the first five came into the light. Sewer Captain White was among them. "'Tis the Sewer guard that let us pass!" he stumbled over the words.

One of the sentries gave words to their collective realization. "'Tis a public hanging." He turned to them, the blood draining from his face.

Before the others could react, the shape of Watchman Cruz stepped up to the rail of the ship and into the light, the same face that was now being seen all over the Sewers.

The entire area of Fairfax Flats iced over into stunned and silent paralysis. The total debilitation quickly spread like a pandemic into every corner of the Sewers. On every street and every corner, Sewer Rats stopped to watch. Back in Dogue Run, it became so eerily quiet that the only sound was the low-pitched humming of the massive magnets that held the gunships aloft.

Johnay turned to the others, his voice numb and shaken. "Hasn't been a public execution since...."

Payne grimly finished his sentence. "Since t'last time this many Sewer Rats were caught runnin'." He bit down on the words. "Since Donnie's dad."

The hulking Imperial gunship just hovered there like an angry parent awaiting a confession before a certain beating. At the rail, Watchman Cruz looked out on the street below and studied the assembled Rats.

Usually encased in the protective bubble of a Lawbroker craft cockpit, this was as close as she'd ever been to the people of the Sewers. The smell was the first thing that hit her. *Like a trash dump,* she thought. *How do they live like this?*

Looking over the decaying structures of Fairfax Flats, she finally blinked. It was like a vast refugee colony when seen up close. She'd always heard the Sewers were mostly full of criminals and savages, as that was the Empire's party line. She'd already seen more in the eyes of Donovan Washington Rush. She saw his eyes again; they were everywhere and upon her at the same time. Their faces were a soiled mix of scared, hateful, and defiant. Cruz blinked at the realization that she saw so much of Donovan's spirit here.

From the perspective of Johnay, Knox, and Payne, this Constabulary display was, at the very least, a show of intimidation and force. At worst, it was about to become an attack on their Dogue Run home and would spell the annihilation of the Brothers and Sisters of the Sword.

Payne turned to the sentries on duty. "Ready boom sticks," he gave the order.

"Wot?" Knox turned.

"We can't abide this, Knox!" Payne glared. "Y'wish t'go down without a fight?" Payne pointed. "Use t'door."

Johnay grabbed the balcony rail to steady himself. He was staying, and when some of the wide-eyed sentries looked to him for guidance, he nodded his agreement with Payne's order. Then, from across the breach between balcony and ship, Sewers and Empire, Watchman Cruz looked over. She and Johnay fell into a strange stare down.

Cruz's elder and one-time partner Monty came to her side. Once a formidable man, broad and fiery, Monty was a caricature of his younger years. A decorated veteran of wars and battles in the Colonies, lands far away, and at sea, time and mileage had long since transformed his once-flowing mane and cool gray eyes to soft and fatherly reflections of a previous life. Monty had been a guide to Cruz, a mentor who was always ready with advice and prodding. It was Monty that eventually got Cruz through her accident, even as the Lawbrokers covered it for her. He taught her to accept the maneuver, bide her time, and wait for the opportunity to use it. Now as Cruz turned to face him, Monty stood ready with more advice.

"I think you've made y'point," he offered.

She turned. "My point?" Cruz was lost in thought.

"Just get on with it," Monty nudged her. "Before you think about it too much." He raised his eyebrows. "Before you give Tarleton or Gage more concerns about you."

The words got Cruz's attention. No matter what she thought now about the Sewers or its children, right and wrong and her place in it all, survival and success depended on duty. She spread her hands out on the rail as if she were much more than a lowly watchman, but before she addressed the Sewers, she took a first shot at her mentor. "I'm not the only one they're concerned about, Monty...." She said it looking straight down, yet she said it as much toward him as to the Rats below. Then, she took a long, pained breath.

"By proclamation of His Magistrate William Frederick the Third," Cruz addressed the streets. "Unless accompanied by Empire Builder Guard and on Empire business, no Sewer Rats may leave the Sewer under penalty of death."

Across on the balcony, Payne turned to the sentries. "Aim fo' t'skunks." He directed his boys to place the officers in their sights.

"'Tis an Imperial gunship." Knox braced. "They'll cut us to ribbons."

"On my signal," Payne ignored him.

"Withdraw!" Knox directed the sentries. "Our cause will neigh be served by suicide!"

The unsure teens looked for a decision. Some maintained their aim.

As unemotionally as possible, Cruz continued her announcement. "No Sewer Rats shall aid or abet other Sewer Rats in any and all attempts to flee…under penalty of death…." She turned and signaled to the platform, where Constabulary Lawbroker guards placed black hoods and ropes about the heads and necks of White and his fellow Militia men. Then, silently, with a smooth motion of her hand, the bodies dropped, bobbed, twitched, and hung still. Then, as if a mere afterthought, the ropes were automatically cut and the bodies dropped to the streets below. More rope then spooled out for the next five. Efficient, technological, and utterly inhuman.

Johnay stood at the rail, his eyes moist and red. "When people speak o' freedom," he half-whispered, "I have t'laugh. No such thing e'er existed; and if it ever does, t'will be hundreds o'years af'er we're dust."

Payne came to the rail and Johnay's side. "Donnie would want this." He braced Johnay's arm. Payne then raised his hand.

"Johnay?!" Knox pleaded and the sentries waited on an order.

"We always have within us t'power to begin t'world anew." Payne looked out on the gunships. "'Tis a message we need t'send.

One that history demands we send. Fo' those future generations Donnie spake of…."

Johnay braced as if hit by a freezing wind. He gave Payne a silent nod. He was now truly ready to join the cause. Payne began to lower his hand as guards pulled Private Catawba and the others to the gallows. The sentries took aim; then, as Payne's hand lowered, they opened fire.

The first bullet found a guard on the deck. He tumbled over the rail and fell into the darkness below. Totally unaware of the attack or that Rats would even dare such a move, the other ship guards calmly looked around. Then, the rest of the initial fusillade followed, and five more of them were cut down. The deck erupted into panic.

A scream of "FREEDOM OR DEATH" rose from the Dogue Run home as the boys reloaded and fired again. The Rats in the street were stunned. Most of them ran for cover. Some stood to watch, so fascinated by the act of rebellion that they were frozen beyond fear.

Just as she began to realize what was happening, a bullet ripped through Cruz's shoulder and, before she took the next, far more deadly bit of metal, Monty pulled her down to the deck. A dead guard then fell onto her, shot through the neck. As the chaos ensued, Cruz glanced out through the rail and found the Dogue Run balcony where dozens of muzzle flashes popped to further announce the attack.

Several of the last five Sewer guards tried to run for the rail, but they were cut down by sleeker and more deadly Lawbroker Barking Irons. Catawba, though, made it to the rail and jumped. He landed hard atop the wreck of an old wagon. Splinters of wood and metal went through his side and took out one of his eyes. He lay there impaled and watched the battle unfold as he waited to die.

Under the deck, at the port-side weapon emplacement, the gunner on duty realized what was happening. He didn't wait for orders and instead returned quick, panicked fire at the Dogue Run building. Sentries fell as Johnay, Knox, and Payne scurried down for cover. The high-powered chain machine gun turned the brick and mortar around them into chipped rubble. The remaining sentries kept firing, and a bullet found its way into the emplacement bubble and silenced the gun and gunner, blood splattered all across the inside of the turret.

"Have they gone mad?" Cruz turned to her wide eyes to Monty.

"We need orders, not exclamations!" Monty grabbed her and yanked her back from the rail just as bullets splintered it to shards. "Turn the rockets on them!"

All at once, Cruz was livid, stunned, and confused. She was about to say yes, but something stopped her. "No, Monty." She grabbed his arm. "We pull back!"

"WHAT?!?"

"I've just added another child to the kills on my ledger, Monty." It came out as a pained half-whisper. "How hard did you work to get me through the first one?"

Monty blinked, "But this is…suicide."

The look in Cruz's eyes hardened to steel. "MONTY! THAT'S AN ORDER!"

He froze as she stood to bark her orders to the rest of the ship. "PULL BACK!" she screamed. "WITHDRAW!"

Monty grabbed her again and she grabbed back. "We can't create an incident."

"We didn't create one!" He pointed into the gunfire as the other two ships swung into attack position. "They did!"

"This is an Imperial issue, Monty. It's no longer a Colonial one. We need orders!" she shouted as she switched her headset mic to internal. "This is Cruz," she screamed. "Break off attack maneuvers, pull back. Repeat, ALL UNITS! PULL BACK!"

Suddenly, the two support gunships turned away and the Imperial gunship just off the balcony began to pull back. The Sentries stopped firing on their own. Could they believe their own eyes? Johnay, Knox, and Payne, too, rose wide-eyed as they emerged from their debris-strewn cover. They knelt there silently. The three ships were leaving.

"They're pullin' out!" Payne half believed his own words.

"'Tis over?" Knox stood up, eyes wide.

As the ships began to climb towards the Empire, a cheer went up across the Dogue Run home. Johnay looked out on the street and the Rats there. Some had rushed over to assist Private Catawba and pull him free. Payne joined Johnay at the balcony rail to watch. He recognized the teen from the filtration gate and was glad to see he escaped, even so wounded.

After a few beats, a much louder cheer went up from the street. It was directed at the Brothers and Sisters of the Sword. These Rats that tolerated and feared them now offered their equally tolerant and fearful support. In moments, the cheer intensified and spread down the streets and alleys of Dogue Run until it shook the very foundations of the Empire above. Johnay realized the implication of it all, the responsibility and trouble of it.

He stood and grabbed the balcony rail. "I'm 'fraid, 'tis only just begun."

Across the Channel and in a more ancient part of the under-city that sat beneath the center of the Empire, another beginning was unfolding. There, holding a small LED lamp ahead of unsteady steps, a hooded figure carefully trundled down a dark, narrow, and rounded catacomb passage. The cramped tunnel was steep; the stones were slick and partly soaked through by centuries of Empire drain water. The masonry was clearly ancient, hand hewn and carefully piled high into the arches. It looked like part of an underground medieval keep. It wasn't far from that.

Deep under the foundation of an old government building that dated back to pre-Imperial times, the well-hidden catacomb descended so far under the foundations of Empire City that it was basically at the same level as the upper Sewers. This dark and foreboding path was known by only a handful of Imperial citizens. It led to a secret society of men and women who considered themselves descended from the original builders, the architects of not only the Empire but of what had come before, maybe even what had gone wrong since. They considered themselves above the laws and regimented rules of the Empire; they thought themselves keepers of a higher order. They were known as the Hellfire Society. They were the secret captains of Empire, the ladies of power, and the people of a truer aristocratic origin.

Above in the Empire, the Hellfire Society was mere rumor or, at best, an urban legend. At worst, it was branded as conspiracy theory. When discussed in a serious form, the secret society was accused of being a notorious den of spies, home base to the eccentricities of the intelligence elite, the ministry of state security—perhaps even more powerful and deadly than the Magistrate himself. Like many urban legends and theories, it was somewhat based in truth.

The hooded figure descended lower and lower down the angled path until the bright flickering light of two large torches filled the base of the tunnel. They guarded a huge oaken door that was emblazoned with a carved relief of a fiery demon and glowing angel locked in a deadly sword fight over a symbolic human heart. As the anonymous robed figure approached the door, two tiny red lasers lit high on the wall and scanned his form. The figure had been watched all the way by technology. The Hellfire Society knew he was there.

"Step forward and declare your status," an electronic voice barked from the door like a Lawbroker interrogating a Sewer Rat.

"Brother Cookham. Number Seventy-Two," the figure said as he lifted his hood. It was Dr. Richard Franklin.

A locking mechanism deep inside the door instantly whirred to life and, one by one, several steel locks disengaged. The massive wooden barrier then smoothly opened, and Franklin stepped through into darkness.

Inside was a vast, dark circular crypt containing a stone forest of forty tight-knit columns, each of which supported a small, vaulted canopy of ceiling. It gave the room the look and feel of an ancient cistern. Franklin passed into the center, where lines etched into the marble floor converged on a spiral staircase that was cut into the stone. On all sides of the great room sat the partly destroyed remnants of statues. The monuments to men were defaced or partly looted or stolen outright. Only one thing was clear: They all faced the center where the stairs were. Franklin seemed to give his anonymous audience a reverent nod as he reached the marble rail atop the spiral stair. Then, he bowed his head and descended into shadow.

The base of the narrow twisting stair opened to a grand, chiseled stone chapel. Lit by flickering torchlight, it too sat at the center of something. The large, domed, temple-like space was surrounded by columns with a dozen or so archways around the sides beyond. Each arch was blocked off by large iron bars. Some of the arches revealed long dark corridors beyond; others were merely alcoves.

The room itself was lush with rich furnishings, antique cabinets, chairs, and couches. Artifacts hung on every wall and lay spread across every table and cabinet. There were stone tablets of strange pictographs or hieroglyphics, obelisks, and small pyramids. There were old boom stick rifles with their accompanying carved-bullhorn powder cases. There were strange books and military medals and busts of mysterious pre-Imperial men among the collection. Beyond those were fragments of battle flags and uniforms that bore a striking resemblance to the Empire's present styles.

At the center of this carefully presented artifice, a wild party ensued. Garishly attired women and men moved through the room, drinking and carrying on. Some nodded at Franklin knowingly, others were too busy to take notice. Franklin smiled as a servant came for his cloak. A woman dressed like a European courtesan in a loose dress of ruffles and satin caught his eye, winked, and rose to greet him with a grab of his shoulders and a seductive kiss.

"Hello, my dear Roxanne." Franklin slipped his hands to her hips and then to the curve of her back.

Roxanne playfully pulled Franklin's hands back to her hips. "When are you going to make an honest woman of me, Dick?" she smirked.

"Why on Earth should I do such a thing?" He beamed back. "Your dishonesty is your best quality."

Roxanne swatted him across the chin and pulled him towards one of the alcoves, where she pried open the bars and shoved him in hard enough that he tumbled, chuckling, onto a cushion-covered couch. Franklin spied a small table nearby that contained glasses of wine and flickering candles. *Roxanne is always prepared.* He smiled inwardly. True to his musings, she pulled a set of side curtains closed and, in one continuous movement, dropped into his lap.

"No time for social discourse tonight?" Franklin chuckled anew.

Roxanne pulled him closer and whispered in his ear. "I've a mind to set a different kind of course, Poor Richard."

"So, this is but a negotiation, then?" Franklin played mock offense. "Is that all I am to you? A convenient consort?"

Roxanne brushed his chin with her fingers and laughed seductively. "What is life at this level of society and power but an exchange of valuable commodities?"

"An ever escalating one, I'm sure." He eyed her.

She giggled again before her demeanor descended into darker tones. "The Capes ambassador de Beaumont has told a friend of ours more of this investigation in Rhodes." She had finally yielded something. "He is very concerned."

Franklin blinked at the gravity of the statement.

"You know, your friend General Goynes is watching you closely."

"Oh?" Franklin's bravado rose in defense. "So says the man from Capes with his own agenda to ply."

"He wishes to speak with you."

"De Beaumont?" Franklin smiled through dark thoughts. He knew Ambassador de Beaumont was as much a spy for the Capes as Franklin often was for the Empire. He also knew the harsh reality that their mutual trade of information would be as much for personal gain and position as it was for country, loyalty, and patriotism.

With many in the Hellfire, such exchanges and barters of information were let out in the open for mutual benefit. So long as one's governmental moves didn't directly threaten war or some other calamity, the men and women of the society thought themselves keepers of a greater and deeper peace. They were the balance for the human nature that sat at the center of it all.

Roxanne was her own fascinating story. A wealthy aristocrat from the Empire's ancient foe, the Capes, she was heir to a royalty that no longer existed, but her ties to the money, gold, and power behind it gave her as much power to wield as any global leader. She preferred to use it in her own way, as a kind of puppet-master power over the others. To Roxanne, her intellect, history, money, and looks were all simply tools. The results were what she lived for, the chess game where she executed the moves of all the pieces on the board. Franklin liked her the better for it. Chess was his favorite game.

Sometime later, Franklin sidled up next to de Beaumont on one of the couches near a collection of old military artifacts. The slight beady-eyed man barely looked at him and, instead, focused on the room and his wine. After a long sip, he only partly turned.

"Amazing how an Empire that sees so much still only sees what it wishes to see." De Beaumont took another sip.

His glass was near empty, so Franklin motioned a servant over to give them both a refill. "The dangers of perception, ambassador." Franklin waited to toast him. "We all possess this weakness."

De Beaumont turned now with a sly smile. He raised his glass back. "It is a common advantage for men such as us, I should think."

"We do not precisely practice the same clandestine vocation, sir." Franklin didn't consider himself a spy at all. It was rather beneath him. "I merely prefer to be informed, no matter the amount of effort involved."

De Beaumont nodded blankly and gulped away half his glass. He didn't believe a word of it. "Are you not worried about General Goynes?" The man from Capes finally eyed Franklin.

"Outside of present revelry?" Franklin eased back into the couch. "I am not involved in his Colonial business." Franklin exhaled as he reclined and thought about Donovan and the boy's beginning adventure in Rhodes. He was lying.

"Then why this investigation and why now?" de Beaumont pressed him further.

"Vanity, I think. There are changes in gubernatorial appointments coming up. This is likely posturing for Goynes to place allies in positions of power, or..." Franklin turned, "maybe the general fancies himself a governor?"

"Will it affect business?" De Beaumont was now fixed on the issue of his own allies in the Colonial Council. It was a skillful turn by Poor Richard.

"Yours, perhaps." Franklin took a drink of wine, turned again, and smiled defiantly.

De Beaumont's insincere smirk creased to a frown.

"The entire affair is still not without concern, however," Franklin continued.

De Beaumont stopped drinking mid-sip.

Roxanne watched from across the room as she rebuffed the approach of two different men. She smiled at de Beaumont's obvious shift in body language. Dr. Franklin was renowned for getting the best of conversations. She'd seen him do it hundreds of times, but still she hung on each decisive turn of word and result.

"The Huaxian market issues are still certainly part of this," Franklin began to think out loud. "Black-Flag profiteering can, if unchecked, cost the Empire a lot of rock." Franklin spread his arm out on the couch; he was fully relaxed now. "However, if they make enough coin off of the Empire by diverting enough of our own profit whilst selling us their own cheaper goods, they could conceivably divert enough treasure to fund a war against us, economically or otherwise."

"Explain otherwise." De Beaumont suddenly eyed him angrily. Franklin had demolished his pretense but stopped just short of accusing the ambassador of treasonous activities.

"An operation to destabilize our Colonial frontier perhaps." Franklin studied his responses. "Tugging at the loyalties and fears of Colonists. A war we shall ironically foot the bill for ourselves."

De Beaumont nodded to himself as he took it in. He was a formidable intelligence operative. Finally, he had his opening. "And if there is a darker cause?" He lingered over his own words as he studied his wineglass.

The question stopped Franklin cold and he sat forward, his arm coming off the couch, his weight shifted to his toes.

"There is a man from my land, who is behind many of these moves," De Beaumont teased. "Behind the Black Markets, the Black-Flag gangs, and even beyond the designs of my own leadership. Leinard is the name," de Beaumont uttered it like it tasted bitter. "Masquerading as a general, he is using cheap, smuggled Huaxian goods to get leverage with the Colonial Council members."

He had Franklin's total attention now and was giving up more of his own agenda. "To what aim?" Franklin turned.

De Beaumont just shook his head, and a smug look took over his usual grouse of an exterior. "A new kind of leverage," he said pointedly.

Slowly, the realization crept into Franklin's mind that this information was going to be costly. "What kind of leverage?" Franklin had to know.

"Land."

The statement caused Franklin's thoughts to grind.

"Land granted by the Colonial Council in exchange for forgiveness of loans and profiteering from cheap goods. Land not given to local merchants and businessmen, but to pay for protection and a share of Black-Flag profit. Land that, in turn, allows the Capes and Huaxia to do something the Empire should have thought of a century ago." De Beaumont's eyes flashed. "Buy into the Colonies, Dr. Franklin, bit by bit, parcel by parcel, until parts of the Empire itself are usurped."

Franklin blinked as his thoughts went inward, de Beaumont's voice muffled into a hush as the blood rushed to Franklin's brain. That was de Beaumont's game. He wanted in on the bounty, ahead of his government, ahead of his own kind.

Franklin nodded. "Yes, I see. Why make money off the Empire by cheating it of profit when you can lend, lease, and rent its own land back to its own people, therefore giving them ownership of nothing and owing of it all?" He blinked again.

"So, what can the Empire do?" de Beaumont pressed. "Seize the land and cause a revolt? If they purchase the land by some ill-served decree, it would feel like a hostile takeover. Only a foreign concern can get away with it under cover of profiteering and petty defiance." The ambassador from Capes sat back. He had control now.

Franklin knew it was time to pay up. "Why are you telling me about this?" he muttered as he massaged his broad chin. "You're betraying the designs of your own country by doing so."

"Mutual goals, Richard." De Beaumont smiled. It was his turn to summon a refill for the two. "If men such as we were to do the same—speculate in the Colonies, maintain vast tracts of Colonial land—together we could block the Huaxians and even my own government and do what this very society we call home portents: We maintain the balance. We put the whole mess in check for the turn of a coin."

Franklin sat back to think it through. The ambassador from Capes had a brilliant plan, no doubt, to work beyond government and international concern. Create a balance of power and, in the process, make a killing. As Franklin thought it through, it sounded better and better and, more than that, it almost sounded necessary, the lesser of two evils.

Once Roxanne noted the conversation had reached some decisive point, she came over, plunked down, and bounced on Franklin's knee. She took his glass and had a drink like petulant child. Then, as the new world spread out before him, the final piece hit Poor Richard like a bolt of lightning.

"General Goynes!" The name tumbled out of Franklin's mouth. "This investigation…"

"…is likely his cover for doing the same, I should think." De Beaumont raised his glass and toasted. "Unless we do it first."

Roxanne tipped the glass to Franklin's mouth and then took her own drink. Franklin's mind was clearly afire. It was a brilliant way to protect and feed off the Empire, perhaps even gain enough power to control it for the better. "We could do this in the Sewers as well," he mused.

"The Empire already owns it." De Beaumont scoffed with a casual hand wave.

"Why not buy it again?" Franklin plucked the glass from Roxanne and set it down. He moved her by the hips to the couch next to him and then stood. "If you were to increase the ability of Rats to pay, you should let them pay, shouldn't you? It would be good for security as well as business." Franklin had turned the tables again.

The hypothetical was dead-on—the very kind of forward thinking and diabolical social engineering that Franklin cherished, the gamesmanship and power-brokering he needed like air to breathe. Suddenly, Donovan Washington Rush wasn't just a way to make things up to Dr. Princeton Rush. The teen was no longer just some tiny experiment in freedom and civic engineering—he was the beginning of something far bigger. He was a revolutionary idea, a new kind of business plan.

Before the conversation could continue further, it was interrupted by a procession of three anonymous hooded men. Two walked in front, dressed in white robes, hoods hung low over their faces like a secretive church liturgy. One slowly swung a cloud of incense into the room using a silver thurible. The other carried a large Paschal candle emblazoned with the stylized red "HF" and triangle of the society. Behind them was another man dressed all in black and red. He kept his head bowed and face hidden and walked with his hands clasped under conjoined sleeves like some kind of wizard or monk. "Gentlemen and ladies—we are starting," the man with the candle announced as, across the way, other white-robed and hooded figures unlocked one of the arched hallways. On cue, the members of the Hellfire Club emerged from every shadow to follow.

The next corridor seemed older still. Unlike the handmade masonry corridors leading to the club and into the crypt, this corridor was entirely hand-hewn into solid rock. It was carefully and artfully vaulted and arched, like a pharaoh's tomb. Down the end of this long secret corridor was yet another chamber, the deepest in the Hellfire Club. It was called the Chamber of the Builders.

The stones inside here were black as sackcloth and only allowed the column-mounted candlelight to illuminate the people and the oak pews in which they sat. Rumor was that they were made from space meteorites and volcanic rock, items forged from the fires of creation both heavenly and earthly.

Once seated in the blackness, it seemed as if the entire gallery was merely floating in empty space, connected to nothing solid. Franklin, de Beaumont, and Roxanne settled into the same row and watched as the hooded procession circled the gallery three times before passing to the front of the chamber where the candle was placed on a nearly invisible black table. The man in the black robe then went to a back wall and ceremoniously flung it open to a glistening cabinet of gold. It caught and amplified the candle-light and the reflected beams hit the room like a sunrise, pouring an orange glow on all the faces. He was plunged into silhouette like a dark force against the light.

Inside the golden altar was a large Hellfire symbol in relief, the same two dueling beings from the main entrance door—and much, much more. There were mathematical symbols, occult and pagan runes, a strange mash-up of history, faith, and mythology. It looked as if the only thing that the Hellfire Society could get completely straight was acting like rakes and spies. The rest seemed confused, complex in its own right, mostly lost to antiquity like recorded history itself.

After a bow to the altar, the hooded priest uncovered his face. Sir Dashwood, the current leader of the Hellfire Society, was a heavyset and handsome-enough man with long, curling brown locks, but it was his eyes that truly set him apart. They were ice gray and large, almost like an albino's. You could not look away from them, but you could not stare into them for long either.

Dashwood approached the table and candle and spread his hands out into the darkness.

"The sun that rises in the east lights the only true path." He paused. "Everything else is darkness or headed into night."

Dashwood's cloaked minions then collected the candles from the surrounding columns and brought them forward. There were holders on the table for each, six on each side, all blocked by an ornate, black metal plate that forced the light back on Dashwood and the altar. The gold light grew blindingly bright and, cut off by the blocking plate, only illuminated the faces of the gallery. Everything else sunk into nothingness. "The origins of our Empire are fraught with darkness," Dashwood continued. "The evil in men's hearts, the forces they cannot escape. The power, the greed, and the corruption in men's souls. We temper that here!" His voice grew louder. "We provide an outlet so that this most natural of human conduct has its proper place to vent. We cleanse the tools of the builders; we remove the filth from the architect's plan and rebuild."

Dashwood's words began to fade into the darkness. Franklin couldn't get his mind from the conversation with de Beaumont. He knew that the land in the Colonies was a key. If indeed the Empire was selling to Colonials to prevent having to move them into the Empire, they were, out of greed and power, creating the means of a vast destabilizing of their own Imperial power. Were people like Franklin and General Goynes thinking the same thing, it had two outcomes: a power grab within the walls of Imperial government or the deadly beginning of a stealthy attack by foreign powers. The only alternative to Franklin outside of purely speculative personal gain was to hold true to the society and cheat the Empire to help maintain it.

10

A WAGER OF FREEDOM

Lawbroker Lieutenant Silas Tarleton clutched at the large arm on Constable Gage's chair and leaned in close as the two men talked in hushed tones. "This incident in NewTown seems to be the tip of the spear," Tarleton probed.

Gage was officious and only slightly interested as he read through some report. "Explain," he huffed halfheartedly.

"There is an Imperial investigation called from the Magistrate's Court about profiteering and smuggling," Tarleton whispered as if his words were leverage.

"Anything I do not know, Tarleton?" Gage nearly yawned. "Would be appreciated."

Tarleton was only setting him up. "Couple that with this group of perhaps fifty or more Sewer Rats making a run for the colony, and at that very instant, the complicit Fairfax Militia guard let them go."

Gage paused and looked up from his reports. Now, he wanted to hear more. "Go on."

"I think it a prelude to foreign invasion." Tarleton's eyes flashed wide.

"Explain." Gage's eyes darted.

"Unrest," Tarleton seethed, "rarely happens of its own accord. It must be provoked, supported, planned..." He paused. "Paid for."

"But the Huaxians and Capes are making more than enough coin in their operations." Gage leaned in close. "Why jeopardize all of that and risk direct Imperial intervention?"

Tarleton took a look through the room of Watchmen and Lawbrokers secretly spying on their conversation. He looked so important now and loved every second of it. "Imperial intervention would infuriate the Colonial Council, who cares little for the Imperial scraps they get now." Tarleton's bravado rose with the success of his point. "You know of my filed reports on the Six Lands of the Sewers. Even if the Capes involvement is simple opportunism, there are tribes and militias in the Sewers that would gladly and violently oppose both Empire and Colonies if provided the opportunity. This discontent could spread across all the Sewer very quickly like a plague for which there is no cure. And if it also spreads fear and unrest to the Colonies?" Tarleton waited for effect. "It would play straight back into the hands of these profiteers and their greater designs."

Gage stopped now and stared deep into his Lawbroker's eyes. He didn't trust him, but he had to listen just the same in order to assess which position to take that would damage him least or profit him most. Still, Gage was tired of this game. In truth, he hated his assignment, and long felt it was a purposeful dead end for him. Working in the Colonies was like a banishment from the Empire. As far as Constable Gage was concerned, any Colonial problem brought to his attention, short of a war, was immaterial. Now it was just about survival.

"You purchased your commission, did you not?" He said it as innocently as he could.

Tarleton blinked. The son of a well-off family, Tarleton had indeed used his inheritance to buy his way into a military position. While he was an accomplished soldier and an asset to Gage, the Constable knew Tarleton worked as much for his own glory as for the Constabulary or the Empire. It mattered little to Gage that Tarleton had cut his teeth in dangerous, undercover Sewer work. Obviously, Tarleton's security was well funded by bribes and coercion.

Constable Gage, conversely, was born in the Empire. His family was aristocracy, and he accepted the job as Constable because it was his duty to do so. Ever since, it nagged at him that he was so far from home and true power. Frustrations with his career and politics had led Gage to walk a delicate line between Colonial law and the gangs, businessmen, and profiteers that helped keep it. Lawbroker Lieutenant Tarleton was an asset to him—perhaps one that may yet pay off—but also one that may possibly blow up in his face.

"What do you propose?" Gage finally tested the waters.

"I wish to go undercover in Prudence Town." Tarleton went for it.

"I don't like the idea." Gage shook his head. "Last thing the Colonial Council, the Huaxians, or Capes will respond to is a bunch of clumsy, trigger-happy Lawbrokers bumbling about. Besides, if we get caught up in this investigation, it would not sit well with this General Goynes."

Tarleton was shot down for the moment but he didn't want to give up. It wasn't his nature or style. He tightly curled his fingers around the arm of Gage's large chair and took a breath. But before he could form his next words, a young watchman rushed up to them with a flashing tablet held in his outstretched hand.

"There's been an attack on the Dogue Run execution party," the young officer blurted.

Gage reached past Tarleton and seized the report. "Attack?" he blurted. "In the Sewers? Impossible." Gage's eyes narrowed as he read. He bit his lip and glanced at Tarleton.

The young officer read it for him: "Seems the Rats opened fire just after the execution."

"How dare they!" Gage seethed.

"Did Watchman Cruz engage?" Tarleton searched the report. Where Gage found insult, Tarleton looked for an opening.

The young officer remained focused on the constable.

"Did she?!?" Gage roared now.

"No, Constable," the watchman stammered. "She, uh, reported that she pulled back to avoid a larger incident."

Gage slapped the tablet back into the man's hands. "Have her report to me the second she arrives."

"Straight away, sir." The watchman rushed off.

Gage eyed Tarleton now. This was escalating fast. He hit some controls on his chair and a comm screen rose up to meet him.

"Send me undercover," Tarleton pressed again. "I can be your eyes and ears in the Colonies and the Sewers."

Gage brushed him off again. "Let me get General Goynes on a call and see what he says about all of this."

In his office at the Ministry of Security, the blue light from a comm screen probed General Goynes's face as he listened to Gage's request for more information.

"What should you do?" Goynes barked incredulously. "Do nothing, of course." The general cast his eyes towards a smug attaché smiling nearby. The younger bureaucrat was enjoying Goynes's power a bit too much, so Goynes wiped his face blank with a sudden stare.

Constable Gage glowered back from the screen. His family still had deep connections in the Empire but not as high as General Goynes. "I don't understand," Gage muttered in disbelief.

In his opulent Ministry office, Goynes smugly eased back into an overstuffed chair. "Thank you for your report."

"It is a request," Gage tried again from Goynes's view screen.

The smug look on Goynes's face soured into a scowl. "May I remind you gentlemen whose investigation this is?" Goynes eyed his attaché and, this time, allowed a small smile between them. "May I also remind you gentlemen where you live and where I live." He then ended the call.

"There is more going on here than our investigation suggests," the attaché offered.

Goynes nodded softly as he pondered the truth. "Summon Mr. Franklin to the Magistrate's Tower for the morning." Goynes scratched his chin. "Ask the Magistrate for an audience first thing."

Back at the Constabulary, Tarleton paced away. "He's cutting us out."

"As is his prerogative. This is going on far over our heads," Gage strategized. "Perhaps his too."

"There is still opportunity here." Tarleton was not about to let this go.

"For whom, precisely?" Gage eyed him. "Bumbling around in the darkness now may end up lighting a fuse."

"Let us not be in competition here, Constable. I have knowledge of the Colonies and Sewers, and you have connections with the Empire. We may both turn a coin if we wager correctly."

Gage took a few more moments to decide. He looked Tarleton over. He was a great asset, a worthy adversary, and a predictably ambitious man. Gage sighed; he was too exhausted to deal with it further and had a ready way to end the conversation. "You're late for your patrol, Lawbroker Tarleton."

The conversation may have been over but Tarleton now suspected that Gage was hiding information. Was he hiding some involvement with the Colonial gangs and profiteers? Tarleton decided to bide his time. If that were true and he discovered it, he'd be made the constable.

Back in the guarded ICU room at Rhodes Colonial Hospital, a metal quill pen dashed across the faded parchment pages of Donovan's mind. Blood and water from the beach at NewTown crept into the margins.

If my own kind wished t'turn a coin on my head, Colonials seemed t'want the whole head first and t'coin af'er. To those o' t'Empire, we Rats are just property 'n' free work. I'd merely gone from prison t'prison, 'n' cage t'cage. Wot was this Colony I'd humped all t'get to but a series o' petty wagers and false enticements? T'was like a distant, forbidden carrot on'a stick, f'ever bobbing out o' reach.

In t'streets of Fairfax, un'er the catwalks of Dogue Run, I'd found t'slidin' scale o' life, t'price o' Rat meat. To a lowly Sewer guard, we were but a means t'survive, 'nuff scratched-out rock t'make a few meals o' needed goods. Wot I beheld in t'Colonies was entirely another matter.

They gazed upon us like cattle, extra coin, a means to a business. My ol' man had wrote 'bout Libertatem, he'd scribbled on about freedom. Pointed me to t'Colonies, but kept much o' wot I'd find from me. Thinkin' if I'd known t'truth o' it, I'd just as soon stay in Dogue Run.

Wot I saw with my eyes af'er we hit t'beach in NewTown was t'last thing I expected. We had more value into ourselves in t'Sewers, more respect and more honour. Least a Sewer guard had his excuse. Seems all t'Colonies had was greed.

Donovan's eyes fluttered open on the last, distasteful image. Then, the pages were gone, and the prison remained.

In the morning light, the dirt, despair, and disrepair of the Colonies was more apparent. Everything in the hospital room—everything in the mix of worn technology and dilapidated building—was covered with advertisements and slogans. Donovan's eyes were strong enough to squint through the ICU window and out into the Colonial streets. The buildings within view were also splattered with LED advertisements and sponsorship. It seemed as if, in the journal of his mind, everything here was for sale.

As Donovan's eyes wandered from the window, he spotted KZ sitting up in her bed, watching. He instinctively flinched but his arms and legs did not move. He was still restrained to the bed. He glanced to the viewing window and the two hulking and well-armed Colonial Council guards. He thought about calling out for safety's sake.

179

KZ stopped him with a hushed and gentle tone. "Feinikesei…."

It took Donovan a few beats to process it. He had a dim recollection of the word and KZ's attempt to kill him in his bed. He looked back at her again and she half smiled. Something was different. *Was it all a dream?*

"You are Feinikesei," KZ said again as she twitched her head back to flip her hair, exposing her intense eyes.

"Whatever." Donovan sighed as he casually let his head hit the pillow. He was dead either way. "They're gonna muster me out, soon as I can stand up for t'rope…yer t'least o' my worry now."

"Feinikesei means phoenix," KZ said with more conviction. "From the ashes." She waited and then continued. "You should be dead but you're not."

Donovan huffed.

"You were meant to live for more than this."

Donovan just silently stared ahead. Out of the cracks and peeling paint above, images of NewTown Beach played from his memory. There was Crispus lifted into the air and crucified like a Roman enemy of the state. There was Carr taking a bomb for him, her body absorbing a thousand shards to bring him here, trapped. Finally, he turned; his eyes were cold and dead on behalf of his Rats.

"Only thing I live for," Donovan hissed. "Is t'get outta this bed 'n' cut yer throat 'fore they stretch mine."

"I can help you here," KZ said flatly. "I can help you in the Colonies."

Donovan began to laugh sarcastically but it hurt too much. Instead, he just clenched his teeth, shut his eyes, and lay back down.

"Did you know that yer kind lives in the original city?" KZ pressed him. "Do you know that's why Boss Dog fears you most?"

Donovan's closed lids fluttered as his eyes darted the darkness. The words rang true. Perhaps KZ knew some bits of the Imperial puzzle, perhaps even a shred or two of things his own father never found.

"So said my father," he finally gave her something.

KZ smiled in relief. She'd finally made some sort of contact. "Smart man." She slipped to the edge of her bed. "Think about that: You walk in the footsteps of kings and queens, yet you live under their feet."

Donovan had enough of it. He looked over now. "Wot do y'want with me?" Donovan Washington Rush was nobody's fool. "Wha's t'game here?"

KZ hesitated.

"Fine. Sod off," he exhaled.

"I tell you, you will not be hung," KZ replied with a misdirect of subject. Still, her words seemed sure and sincere. "I heard the watchman say it." She nodded. "Somebody very powerful's looking after you."

The comment shifted Donovan's focus inward again as he put some of the fragments and pieces together. *Did KZ know about the Empire pin? Had Dr. Franklin from the Magistrate's Tower been there? Did more people know about him?*

The focus of Donovan's eyes moved about the room. KZ caught the meaning of the inner betrayal.

"In the drawer beside your bed." She motioned with her head. "Look."

Donovan strained against his binds and was barely able to slide to drawer open far enough to see. The pin was there but his father's book was gone.

"Lady watchman mentioned you might be bombproof." KZ played the ally now. Then, she noticed that he was fixed on the drawer. Something was wrong.

"Somethin' got your goat?"

"Nothing." Donovan shut the drawer as he tried to hold back an empty cavern of questions and fears.

KZ waited a few moments more before breaking the silence. "Do you even know how these colonies really work, my little Sewer Rat?"

"I've an idea," Donovan hissed. "Y'are kept in competition for favor o' t'Magistrate 'n' his Empire, climbing all o'er each other like rats in an endless maze."

KZ met his glare and continued for him. "Never getting quite enough but just enough to get by. Which makes the few and strongest rats take it by force, or find shortcuts to get it."

"So, now we're t'same?" Donovan's eyes flared with anger.

"It was nothin' personal." KZ swallowed her own anger at her lost gang members. "The price of business."

To Donovan she seemed genuinely conflicted. She was, but it was still a conflict between loss and gain.

Donovan knew his Sewer Rats were invaders in Colonial eyes—that Colonists would consider them a danger not just to Colonial interests but also as they were illegal lawbreaking enemies of the Empire and, as such, exposed any friendly Colonists to the same punishments of death and imprisonment.

But KZ was more human suddenly, and to Donovan, her hard beauty and mystery were enticing. A former deadly foe turned friend or perhaps coconspirator. His intellect pulled him out of his fanciful thoughts.

"You tryin' t'say that we're e'en somehow?"

"Right about now, little Rat," KZ's eyes almost smiled, "I'm in as much danger for talking to you as you are for comin' here. Besides," she sat back, "Rhodes Colony is fulla ledgers and balance books. Each Colony fighting for their own tiny profits, but who truly profits?"

"T'Empire."

KZ nodded. "And they do it by us starving each other out for their favor." KZ sat back in her bed as one of the Colonial Council guards came by the window to look in. She quickly laid her head back and looked up at the ceiling.

"You're under Colonial Council guard now," she said to the ceiling. "The governor's men." She let it sink in. "Not local Mules, not Lawbrokers, and not Imperials." She waited for Donovan to react and for the guard, now satisfied that all was quiet, to walk away. "Empire's afraid to touch you. Imagine that."

"Worse than death." Donovan thought about it all: the missing book, Empire pin, and dead escape party. He was alone, but like his father, he thought, free inside his mind.

"We're not so different." KZ sat back up. The words rang true. "Sewer Rats patrolling and terrorizing their own. Others profiteering and making deals with Empire Mules on the Black Market for a few extra rocks. What did it truly serve but, eventually, as the money went up and up, on a wing and a prayer, to only truly serve the Empire." She waited for it to all sink in. "Think about that." She eyed him. "The better the Rat, the more powerful the Imperial."

Donovan's father taught him well. "So now, instead o' tryin' t'cut my throat, you're offering me an accord?"

KZ waited on a yes.

Donovan preferred the Sewer version of what she could go do with herself. "Go to rut!" he snapped.

KZ's eyes turned to fire and her whole face bent into a crooked snarl. "Suit yourself." She eased back onto her pillow again. "I'm the one getting paid for every kill last night. I'm the one walking out of here," her tone descended to a demeaning huff, "Empire Builder."

Later that morning in Rhodes Colony, a low cold front moved in from the Channel, plunging NewTown and then Prudence Town into a thick fog and steady mist. Towards Prudence Town, the mist picked up the neon adverts and messages and filled the air with soft flickering colors that hid the unrest and cutthroat world beneath. An ill-serviced Magistrate's crown logo flickered on the side of the vast Constabulary building

Bandaged shoulder and wounded career, Watchman Lee Cruz stood under the chair and judgment of Constable Gage. The elder Monty, like he had in better times, stood by her side. Gage spent a full minute to just look down at them quietly and then, with the whole room watching, stood from his perch, stepped down, physically pushed Monty away, and circled Cruz.

"They took us by surprise...we had no option," Cruz thought to speak first.

Gage stopped by her face and hovered. He looked like he wanted to strike her. Instead, he turned and went to pacing, playing to the room and perhaps any other Imperial informants that might be there. "A goddamn uprising in the Sewers and a bunch of runaway Rats...and one of my watchmen, mucking it all to hell?"

"They had hundreds of homemade weapons."

Gage stopped in front of her again. This time, he couldn't hold back. "SPEAK WHEN DIRECTED!" The hot spit hit her face. Gage took two breaths and straightened out his uniform.

"Homemade?" He turned and looked at Monty. "Rocks, sticks, and damn slingshots, too, no doubt."

"Rifles, sir," Monty offered in Cruz's defense.

Obsessed by the defense by both Watchmen and Sewer Rats, Gage hadn't yet bothered to go through the situation report fully. He stopped hard. "Rifles of this sort in the Sewers are Black-Flag!" He turned to the room and caught Lieutenant Tarleton's eyes. "You could have arrested the lot of them for that alone. Hung them, even!"

Cruz held her shoulder towards the constable. "They were shooting back, sir." Gage glared but waited for more. "Are you suggesting that I slaughter them," she paused, "on my own authority?" She had a point, and with things already so uncomfortable with General Goynes, even Gage recognized that she may have done him a favor by not escalating the event.

Still, Gage wanted to at least publicly cover his tracks with his own office. "How do you think this looks on the street? In the Colonies AND the Sewers?" He flailed his arms as he returned to pacing. "The Colonial Constabulary turning tail? Armed Rats! We're security for the blasted Colony, Cruz!"

"It looks better than them mustering out an entire patrol." Cruz was right and she knew that Gage had to cede the point.

"There were a hundred of them." Monty felt emboldened enough to join in again. "Maybe more. They might have shot us out of the sky."

Another salient point. Still, Gage played the public display well; his flanks were covered. "I've contacted General Goynes from the Magistrate's Court for an opinion." He calmed his tone, but Cruz and Monty shared a glance just the same. If things went bad here, this would be the end of them. "He said," the constable continued, "that he was aware of the situation and will consider the matter further."

Now, Cruz knew for sure that the Empire had to be watching her Rat, but why? All she could think of was that no matter where he went, as long as that pin was on him, she may be the only Colonial who knew about it.

Gage snapped her from these worries with a raised eyebrow and pointed and immediate taunt. "Let's hope he doesn't ask to stretch your necks."

Crude boxes, backpacks, and crates filled the central meeting room of the Brothers and Sisters of the Sword. Knox and Payne rushed back and forth, supervising sentries and other teens as the contents of the Dogue Run home were packed up. The boys were fleeing, running into hiding in the gang-filled Sewer town of Auldville past Auld Way and near the Black-Flag Perimeter Five.

Knox brought up piles of old secret books and texts, which were merely fragments and bundled pages of ancient and mostly complete volumes. Payne packed maps and papers; the sentries boxed up supplies, candles, food, and weapons. Johnay sat at the center of it all at the now-cluttered central table. He was writing in a journal, the way Donovan used to write in his father's book. Johnay wanted to keep the flame burning but was taking a far different tack than Donovan. After being part of the bloody and failed escape to the Colonies and witnessing the carnage of the Colonials killing his friends almost as an afterthought, Johnay looked into the cause.

In t'earliest ages o' this world, absolute power seems to have been t'universal form o' governance. Kings, magistrates, 'n' a few o' their great counselors and captains held a cruel tyranny o'er t'people, as if they were but mere pack animals that carried them 'n' their engines to war. As I sit here still wiping the blood from m'face, tryin' to wash t'horrors I've seen from my mind, it b'comes clear how much I've missed.

Wot were t'Colonies? Wot indeed are t'Sewers but an endless pyramid o' tyrants, all trickling down from t'apex o' power, each level down as cruel 'n' detached by self-interest 'n' greed as t'next. Only thing that seems to dwindle is the scope and profit of t'repressive deed. But t'power 'n' control seem unchanged fro' t'top; the cruelty remains unabated. This is t'true product 'n' profit of t'Magistrate's domain.

T'poor people here in t'Sewers, 'tis true, have been much less successful than the great. We've ne'er found opportunity to form a union 'n' exert any strength at all. 'Tis the true power o' tyranny, to keep us in survival, competition, 'n' squalor—by design. Wot o' rights? Wot right does a Rat have to freedom? Wot right does a Magistrate have to absolute control? If Magistrate has t'might to take rights, then, by sheer natural law, we have t'right to take them back. If we all spring from t'same divine or universal source, then we all possess the same right.

This all bein' sed, swift 'n' deadly punishment's coming, but I no longer fear it. 'Tis a moral matter now, a legal one. This Empire 'n' all it touches 'tis no longer wot we fight against as a symbol, 'tis illegal, against humanity and immoral.

Yesterday, I was a boy looking fo' freedom 'n' b'lievin' in dreams. Today, I've joined t'rank o' soldier, 'tis a fight now, a just cause that binds us. If t'injustice we tasted in *t' Colonies runs as deep as t' Empire, 'n' I b'lieve it does, then we fight fo' t' rights of e'ry one suppressed, from the filth 'n' despair o' t' Sewer straight to t' highest ivory tower o' t' Empire.*

11

MR. FRANKLIN'S FIRES

FIVE HUNDRED MILES UP and away in Prudence Town, Watchman Lee Cruz read from a different book: Donovan Washington Rush's book, the words of Dr. Princeton Rush.

> If any generation ever possessed the right to dictate the mode by which the world should be governed forever, it was the first generation that existed. And as that generation did not do so, no succeeding generation has the authority. The illuminating and divine principle of the equal rights of humanity (which has its origin in the Maker of all things) relates, not only to the living individuals, but to the generations to come. Every generation is equal in rights to the generations that preceded it by the same rule that every individual is born equal in rights with their contemporary.

Every history of the creation and every account, whether from the lettered or unlettered world, however they may vary in their opinion or belief, all agree in establishing one point: the unity of human kind, by which I mean that all are of one degree and consequently that all are born equal and with equal natural rights, in the same manner.

Therefore, every child born into the world must be considered as deriving their existence from God. The world is as new to him or her as it was to the first who existed, and his or her natural right in it is of the same kind.

Cruz dropped the book to her coffee table and looked around her small but comfortable apartment. The trappings and salary of her watchman career were sufficient to maintain her life, but sufficiency was just that: a daily grind, a constant struggle against making do and planning for a future. It always seemed to her that some other force was holding the reins to her life. She knew it was, of course, but had looked away from the truth of it long ago. Now she realized that she'd always been conditioned to accept her fate.

She was always busy with a case, the next item on an official agenda, the sufficient power to provide the illusion of making a real difference. *Trappings,* she thought. *What are Lawbroker Tarleton's trappings but just that? Constable Gage? What is going on in Empire City that requires watching Donovan Washington Rush? Is there some plan from on high to smash a rebellion in the Sewers? Is there a plan afoot to destabilize the Colonies for some political gain? Is there something far darker and momentous at work?* No matter the mental gymnastics, Cruz was left with a bitter set of thoughts.

She knew that the Constabulary had protected her after her accident...or had they allowed it to gain some leverage over her? Did they encourage Monty to pull her along? Was he really ever the friend she accepted him as? Worse still, were her actions now, reading this book and hiding information, just confirmation of their all-knowing ability to control their own? Or again, was there something darker lurking? Was she being watched out of fear or in order to gain insight into the mind of a potential revolutionary? The trappings closed in again. Cruz agreed with the book, and she agreed with Donovan's struggle for freedom, a freedom she herself thought she, too, didn't have. *What have I gotten myself into? The trappings of a rat,* she thought.

Suddenly, a rage welled up inside Watchman Lee Cruz as she placed the book on the table and rose to pace. She passed her shelves of books and small curios and mementos of life, her decorations from her career and education. She took the next step to her tablet computer and crossed the line from officer of the law to budding rebel, secretly activating an electronic frequency trace on Donovan's Empire pin. He was still in Rhodes Colonial Hospital, but for how long? Time was running out, but for what? *Trappings.* She sank back onto the couch and just stared at the blinking dot. *So much hope,* she thought. *So much trouble, danger, and possibility in this tiny, electronic blink of a life.*

A window opened on her screen. It was text a message from Monty. It was accompanied by a request for a video call.

"What in hell do you think you're doing?" Monty's words forced the air from her lungs.

After hesitating on letting the video connection open, she answered. His worried face met hers.

"It's way past your bedtime, old timer," Cruz said, hoping Monty wasn't referring to Donovan's signal.

He was. "What file is that?"

Cruz stumbled over what was left of her breath and words.

"You're damn fortunate that I found you before Internal Security," he added pointedly.

"You were watching me?" Cruz was angry and felt violated.

Monty scowled. "I was your partner, Lee. We still share the network. To protect and to monitor, right?" His expression softened into a smirk. "I'm doing both."

Cruz relaxed. Monty could have just turned her in by now. Maybe he really was on her side. Maybe it was an alliance of impending doom. After all, with the botched execution, they were in the same Imperial boat.

"Go to sleep, Monty," she tried to kid.

"This isn't funny, Lee," he persisted. "I need an explanation and I think you may need a drink."

She blinked. "One?" Then, she tried to take a breath and rubbed her face. "I need sleep."

"Now." Monty stared. "Meet me in NewTown."

It was the location of the Rat incursion. Was Monty looking for the whole story or was he looking to dig for even more? Or was he just looking for a piece of the action if there was any?

"The White Horse on Marlboro."

Before Cruz could agree, Monty hung up.

Monty chose well. The White Horse was the oldest tavern in the Colonies and a favorite haunt of many members of the Colonial Council. It almost seemed like a test to see if Cruz had some other Colonial business that might make the location uncomfortable for her. The White Horse was a simple place—wood and plaster, colonial style. It would fit in on the streets of the Sewers or the Colonies, and indeed there was that quality about it. The windows were small and far apart, the inside dining area lit as much by lamp as by light from outside.

Monty sat across from Cruz, sipping a beer and eyeing her. "You know, Gage asked me to watch you," he began cautiously.

"That pompous windbag!" Cruz suddenly put down her glass of whiskey. "Did you write me up?"

"How much have we been through?" he groused.

"Did you write me up?" she pressed to see if she was in deeper trouble than she already thought.

Monty smiled playfully, took a drink, sat back, and shook his head. "You better trust me, Lee." He eyed her. "I might be the only real friend you have."

Cruz took a long sip from her glass and stared back. She still didn't know Monty's game or even if there was one. But one thing was for sure—she wasn't going to hand him one, either, so she took a few moments to compose her thoughts. Monty, for his part, took it as a few moments to craft a tale.

"The runaway Sewer Rat had that pin," Cruz gave him the truth of it. "I haven't told Tarleton or Gage." She glared at him, expecting a fight.

His expression softened. "I've never even seen a Magistrate's pin in person."

Cruz smiled now and pulled her tablet to the tabletop. She opened the file of the pictures she took and clandestinely showed Monty an image of the pin in the palm of her hand. When Monty recoiled from the picture so as not to be caught looking at it, Cruz relaxed. Monty was here because he was scared.

"Did you run it?" He blinked.

"Wiped clean." Cruz shook her head. "But it's trackable from the other end, meaning somebody's keeping tabs on our little Rat."

"Our?" Monty backtracked.

"Is now." She grinned as she relaxed more. Trouble had company now.

"Somebody in the Magistrate?" Monty lowered his voice to a whisper.

Cruz shrugged. "But I have the frequency. So now I can track him, too, if I can break the encryption."

Monty sat back as his wheels spun to a thoughtful stop. He put down his beer and leaned in closer. "That's why you pulled out the transport instead of counterattacking. You didn't want to end this yet." The thought frightened him, but his eyes betrayed the growing hint of mischief. It was the kind of look that Cruz had only seen years earlier, from a younger man. It was from a time when Monty was a fiery sort and had more hope for his life and career.

Cruz spotted the smile and nodded to it. She once had the same fire and hope. "This could be big, Monty," she added. "Our chance to get to Empire City, to High Town. Out from under this life."

Monty looked over at the Colonial businessmen dotting the room and perhaps the Council members present too, all dining and drinking, and thought about how well off they were, but Monty knew it was mostly illusion and pretense. Cruz was talking about a life far beyond the Colonies, anyway.

"If we could catch somebody in the Magistrate dealing directly with the Sewers," she rolled her whiskey glass between her palms, "we'd be heroes...we 'd be bombproof."

Monty thought about it. "What if this news gets to Gage?" he worried aloud.

"It won't," she assured him, as much as she tried to convince herself. "They've pushed you down harder than they ever pushed me, Monty. This is for you as much as anybody. Besides, you really think Gage and Tarleton are any different? What do you think they'd do if they were us?"

Unlike the gray and misty Colonies, daybreak over the Magistrate's Tower meant beams of sunlight streaming through the metallic jewels and glass of the immense and sprawling structure. The original Builders of the Empire had carefully planned it this way. The tower and its portals and reflective surfaces had been positioned to bounce and channel the morning light west as if spreading the power to the people there during the morning hours—then, as the glowing disc of the sun passed to the west, it was also set up to return the same light east. It was as if the government alone bestowed light and life on various bits of the city as the sun traveled the sky. The inference was clear: the sun never fully set on the Empire until it set upon the whole of the world.

Just under the Magistrate's Chamber at the apex of the vaulted arch sat the Magistrate's private Audience Theater, accessible from the Magistrate's Chamber via a hidden spiral staircase that could be accessed through a secret door behind the throne. The Magistrate's Theater was another cavernous, ornately gilded room containing a long central table surrounded by a dichotomous mix of old statues, paintings, and massive state-of-the-art video walls. Dim and haze-filled scenes from the Sewers played on the Magistrate's screens. Flashes of the hanging and the attack by Donovan's Brothers and Sisters of the Sword were followed by the three fleeing Imperial gunships.

Tight in the bonds of his royal regalia and tapping a pale finger on the polished arm of his ornate gold and obsidian chair, His Magistrate William Frederick the Third shifted uneasily. The young monarch could not seem to find a comfortable position. At one point, he seemed to look down at this alternate throne as if contemplating its punishment. Then, he sighed, pulled a few strands of flaxen hair from his gray-green eyes, and stared ahead. Three men—Dr. Richard Franklin, General Goynes, and the semi-corpulent and robed Lord North, the Empire's prime minister—sat before him.

"Mr. Franklin." The Magistrate began the meeting in a deceptively detached voice. "You've spent time in the Colonies and accompanied undercover Lawbrokers on patrol in the the Sewers."

Franklin nodded. "I have, my Lord."

"You have, shall we say, some first-hand knowledge of the," William Frederick paused on a bitter-tasting thought, "rodent problem." He then looked away. "So, what do you make of this... situation?"

Goynes and North turned their eyes to Franklin. The doctor quickly surmised that while the Magistrate may indeed be simply looking for advice from one of his most trusted sources, Goynes and North clearly had different agendas.

"It's not a surprise," Franklin responded offhandedly and confidently as he sat back in his chair.

"Explain that remark." Goynes seized at nothing of note.

Franklin slowly eased out of his chair and stood, forcing both king and country to follow him about the room. Franklin walked to the screens, still flashing images of carnage and rebellion. "Sewer Rats have always been promised a shot at betterment in exchange for their labor as Empire Builders." He stopped on images of the attack on the gunships and turned. "But hardly any of them are ever really allowed to stay unless proven invaluable and trustworthy as house servants." He took a cleansing breath as he shifted points. "The ones we catch are given dangerous work; the ones that try and stay or refuse are executed." Franklin moved onto the hanging scene before turning back for the long conference table. "Meanwhile," Franklin turned further to carefully address the Magistrate directly, purposefully ignoring both North and Goynes. "The Colonials are promised a shot at living here, but less than two percent of them make it," he waited a beat, "even though their trade and industry generate over seventy-seven percent of the total domestic commerce and income for the Empire."

Franklin eased back into his chair and intertwined his fingers across his chest. "It was only a matter of time before some part of an already strained system cracked."

The whole table seemed to shift. The Magistrate and Prime Minister North made momentary eye contact. General Goynes, partly out of friendly competition but also on suspicion and political preservation, tried to stop his friend's momentum.

"May I remind you, sir," the general directed his eyes to Franklin, "that as the former minister of cultural affairs, you were the one who reorganized the Colonial Council to keep order so as not to adversely affect the prices across the Empire."

Franklin took it in with a smug nod, but Goynes persisted.

"You also suggested the Empire Builder program to offer hope as a means of control and protection from dissent." The general then leaned back and studied the table to see if his volley had found a mark.

If it did, it wasn't with Franklin. "Perhaps there are other things we need to protect ourselves from now, General Goynes," Franklin responded coolly.

"Such as…?"

"Not my decision to say." Franklin didn't flinch as he eyed the Magistrate. "Nor yours, General."

The exchange created a harsh silence, and His Magistrate William Frederick the Third clearly enjoyed the chess game. Prime

197

Minister Lord North did not. He had little patience for chess and less so for disorder.

"We are debating the disposition of armed savages." He turned to his leader. "Nothing more. We should send in an Imperial battalion and make an example of them immediately. Swift justice is the only solution capable of quelling such insurrection."

It was clear that Lord North was just warming up, but His Magistrate would have none of it. He calmly waved his thin hand in the air to silence the second most powerful man in the Empire.

"There is always time for that, Lord North." The Magistrate softened his voice into a net as if to catch and cushion the tension instead of stop it cold.

Even in his distance and imperial vanity, William Frederick the Third was well schooled and masterfully smart. Perhaps even in the deepest caves and alcoves of his mind, he knew of the untenable nature of his own monarchy and maybe even the basic injustice of it, but the alternative would see custom and history out of power. Power was all he and his predecessors knew. It defined them to the point that they'd institutionalized it.

"I am simply asking the good doctor his opinion, Lord North," the Magistrate stifled a yawn. "This is not the time nor the place for gamesmanship."

"Yes, my lord," North grumbled as General Goynes sat back to study the dynamic. Was the Magistrate himself running a game of his own? Was Franklin being set up? William Frederick was excruciatingly hard to read.

Franklin jumped into the silence. "I suggest caution with all parties involved," he exhaled. "These are tenuous times. We have other powers looking to get their goods into the Empire and past the taxes and embargoes we put on them."

"Who?" Goynes challenged him, not expecting him to have a ready answer.

"The Capes for one, obviously." Franklin eyed Goynes. It was a direct shot across his bow and his investigation. He put his information from fellow Hellfire spy de Beaumont to good use. "The black markets and gangs in the Colonies are more than happy to speculate and fix prices for profit on our own colonial-produced goods, and the Council makes a handsome wage looking the other way for their and our mutual benefit. But clearly, cheaper goods from elsewhere, unchecked, could quite easily cripple our entire economy."

The Magistrate and Lord North were suddenly caught in Franklin's web. Were this true, as Franklin and de Beaumont had discussed, an outside power could severely damage the Empire through destabilizing trade or commerce itself via a flood of cheaper goods.

"But we could just shut down the ports," North insisted. "Decree an embargo. Weed out the foreign profiteers and stop the whole of the mess before it begins."

Goynes jumped in. "I am on this trail already."

Franklin cut them both off. "There is another matter." He waited on their full attention. "Closing the ports would only starve the starving."

"Explain that." The Magistrate's cold eyes blinked.

"Properly alarmed by rising violence in the Sewers and the use of more outward Imperial force," Franklin continued, "both the Colonials and the Rats might suddenly become more inclined to unite in their own spheres...maybe even...listen far more to voices outside the Empire?"

"I see." The Magistrate began to tap his finger again.

"Surely you are not suggesting that we placate lowly animals!" Lord North interjected.

"They simply want the chance at freedom they were promised, Lord North." Franklin stared him down.

"By *your* programs." Goynes tried to pile on his friend.

"As *Empire Builders*, Mr. Goynes!" Franklin thundered back. "The very program that this body never fully implemented." His eyes flashed with anger, then settled down.

"These are your fires that burn, Mr. Franklin," North added as he gestured to the chaotic images flashing across the screens.

"Yes, I suppose, in a sense, they are." Franklin took a cautionary tone. "But putting a fire out by force often leads to more secondary conflagrations. But keeping them burning," he raised a finger, "in a controlled sense, provides warmth and perhaps even a false sense of security."

"So," the Magistrate turned to him, "you wish to partly reward these actions?"

"These people paid with their lives, my lord." Franklin lowered his voice. "It is to be expected." His eyes turned towards Donovan Washington Rush on the screen. "And in some sense, admired."

"I caution you, sir," North seethed. "Do not make this about freedom."

"Really?" Franklin sat back again. "I wonder. What price have we truly paid for our own?"

Goynes and Lord North stared at their leader. The Magistrate wanted to hear more but also didn't wish to alienate his own cabinet.

"Alright." The leader of the Empire took a breath. "This is quite enough, Mr. Franklin."

Goynes and North turned satisfied eyes towards Franklin.

But before they could silently gloat, their Lord and leader added more. "And enough from the both of you as well." The Magistrate then brought his hands to his chin in a prayer-like and contemplative maneuver.

"Make no mistake," William Frederick the Third began, "no matter the course, we must act quickly and decisively, as Lord North states. The majority of those in the Colonies and even those in our Sewers obey our laws and remain loyal to our Empire and its rules. But petty profiteering oft turns to economic skirmishes, which, in turn, lead to outside opportunism." He looked at Goynes. "Escape from station can turn into a refugee problem and all that accompanies it," he then added to North. "Insolent revolt can, if unchecked, turn to revolution." Then he eyed Franklin. "But as Dr. Franklin states, I also do not think facing the problem with brute force and violence the correct path."

The Magistrate then eyed the screen where the Sewer attack on the gunship was frozen. "This incident in the Sewer, this watchman?" He waved his hand for the information.

"Cruz," Goynes fed him.

"Should be commended for her restraint." The Magistrate paused. "Promoted even, to full Lawbroker."

Lord North's eyes opened into wide protest. "But...."

"We are not an Empire of barbarians," the Magistrate chided his prime minister as Franklin smirked at Goynes. "Placing troops in the Sewers and Colonies would only inflame the spirit of revolt. As General Goynes insists, we may have created the spark with the programs brought forth by Mr. Franklin, but perhaps we have simply not engineered nor administered these programs to our advantage."

Goynes finally shook his head at his friend, ceding the small power struggle.

"A middle ground—even in mere appearance—would be the proper course," the Magistrate continued. "The veneer of restraint may, in time, lead to passive acquiescence and perhaps even a growth in loyalty."

Lord North began to speak again. The Magistrate again cut him off. "I am extremely anxious to prevent, if possible, the effusion of the blood of my subjects, and the calamities that are inseparable from a state of war. Proper moves will show the people of both the Colonies and Sewers the traitorous and dangerous views of their anti-Empire leaders. Remaining temperate in the offering of middle ground will show that serving the Empire is the only and best course available."

With Goynes and North now stunned and even compelled to silence, Franklin again jumped into the void. "If we let the Colonies further unify, make the council stronger and more connected to us, perhaps there will be less corruption to deal with as well."

"Or more centralized corruption," Goynes huffed.

"That will be yours to investigate, John." Franklin threw him a nice bone. "Even in such corruption, it would be our corruption to administer and therefore, the lesser of two evils."

Goynes nodded. He took the offering as a clear compromise.

The Magistrate smiled for the first time.

"Let them assemble." Franklin gained momentum. "Let them organize, let them fight it out for more profit, more perceived freedom, but on a higher level of payment to us. If the Capes or the Huaxians have to get past a stronger and more unified Colonies and Council, they will have to buy their way in at a far higher price and therefore have a much harder time avoiding our tariffs and restrictions."

"Yes!" The Magistrate pounded the table. "Make them more able to self-govern, so long as they show more fealty to the Empire."

"And about these renegade Rats?" North growled.

"Let a few of them house in the Colonies." Franklin smoothed his lapels. "It would be seen as a gigantic step up in rights and power. Let them work and pay fees to the Council and Empire. Then, after a time, let them go back and give hope to their kind."

"And who chooses them?" North shot back. "And on what basis?"

"Let those loyal in the Sewer Guard Militias decide." The Magistrate rubbed his chin. "Another Imperial carrot!"

"It would invite more profiteering, Your Magistrate," Franklin cautioned. "It will make the Sewer Militias more powerful and greedy. It would be tantamount to a form of slave trade."

"But it would maintain order and provide hope." His Magistrate pulled on his chin now. He had sold himself. "Yes, let them work, let them make a coin, let them advertise our noble brand, and win their little battles to prevent a later war."

He then turned to Franklin. "I will dispatch you to the Colonies at once, as special envoy to the entire Colonial Council. I wish a full plan for your efforts by the morrow."

Franklin stood, bowed to a glowering Lord North, and winked at an outfoxed General Goynes, then departed after tipping his hat to his king. "At your service, my lord."

As soon as Franklin was gone up the spiral stair, Lord North fixed a glare on the space where he had been sitting. "One can only wonder," North spoke at the empty chair, "what will rise from the ashes of Mr. Franklin's fires."

Goynes turned to the Magistrate as well. "I don't trust him," he added.

"I do," the Magistrate said flatly. "But just in case you are right in your suspicions, I have a remedy," the Magistrate added before touching one of the rings on his hand. It was a control for a door at the back of the Audience Theater. Benny, the kid from the Empire Builder transport who'd helped Donovan hide his book. stepped through.

"My lord." Benny bowed to the Magistrate as Goynes and North exchanged a look.

"Gentlemen, this is Mr. Benedict Waterman King." The Magistrate got up from his chair and led the teen to the table and a chair. "Born in Conn's Colony, right between York and Rhodes."

Benny sat, and the Magistrate put his hands on the boy's shoulders. "His parents were born in the Colonies, too, before his father fell out of favor, causing their banishment to the Sewers. He is an Empire Builder now. One of the most loyal ones I've seen. He always wanted to be a doctor, you know. He studied on his own and one day, not but two months ago, he recognized the smell coming from a cup of tea brought by one of my own servants." He eyed his council. "It was poison. Let's just say, I believe he can be very helpful to my plan."

"Your plan?" North blinked.

The Magistrate turned and paced to a bank of windows at the far side of the room and looked out over his Empire. "Mister Franklin is right about one thing. We cannot act too quickly. We need to see how far this problem goes before we move. We need to find out just who is involved in this growing insurrectionist cancer on our shores."

He paced back to his chair and sat. "Let it grow a bit, take a culture of it, put it under a spyglass, then, like any good practitioner of medicine, rip, cut, and burn it out from every corner where it exists…completely and ruthlessly."

Goynes and North just took it all in. Across the table, Benny shot a cocky smile their way. *Goynes,* thought the boy, *is as dangerous as he is ambitious. This may not end well.*

To be continued in…

REVOLUTION EMPIRE
BOOK TWO:
THE WILD COLONIALS

ABOUT THE AUTHOR

Rob Travalino is a Telly, Effie, Gemini, and Emmy Awards winner. He has been a creator, screenwriter, author, and marketing expert for twenty-plus years and has overseen, or contributed to, the development and realization of some of the world's most powerful and lasting franchises.

As an independent content developer, Rob co-created and story-edited the Gemini Award–winning Alliance Atlantis TV show *Dragon Booster*, which aired on Toon Disney, and developed the Emmy Award–winning teen property *Growing Up Creepie* for Mike Young Productions and Discovery TV. As a marketing executive, Rob oversaw the development of fully integrated and multi-platform content and brand initiatives for Lucasfilm, Hasbro, Warner Brothers, and many others. He also helped relaunch both the *Transformers* and *Batman* franchises for kids TV. In 2022, Rob co-wrote the gripping memoir *Over the Wall* for Post Hill Press. The book explores former NYPD Lieutenant Kevin M. Hallinan's influential career in law enforcement and counter-terrorism.

A member of the Directors Guild of America, Rob continues to consult on narrative content across the media spectrum. He graduated magna cum laude from Iona College in New York, with a focus on broadcasting and journalism.